With the Night Mail

WITH THE NIGHT MAIL
A STORY OF 2000 A.D.

and

"AS EASY AS A.B.C."

by

RUDYARD KIPLING

introduction by **MATTHEW DE ABAITUA**

afterword by **BRUCE STERLING**

—

HiLoBooks
powered by **Cursor**
Boston, MA *and* **Brooklyn, NY**
2012

Introduction © Matthew De Abaitua 2012
Afterword © Bruce Sterling 2012
Foreword © Joshua Glenn 2012

The text of *With the Night Mail* (1905) follows the edition published by Doubleday in
1909; "As Easy as A.B.C." (1912) follows the text as it appeared in the collection *A Diversity
of Creatures*, published in 1917 by Doubleday, Page. Both texts are in the public domain.

Library of Congress Control Number: 2012931028
ISBN: 978-1-935869-52-8

Cover illustration © Michael Lewy 2012
Cover design by Tony Leone, Leone Design
Interior typography & layout by Matthew Battles

Printed in the United States of America

HiLoBooks
A project of HiLobrow.com, a critical-culture website
founded by Matthew Battles and Joshua Glenn.
For more information, visit HiLobrow.com/HiLoBooks

Powered by Cursor

Distributed by Publishers Group West

10 9 8 7 6 5 4 3 2 1

FOREWORD

SEVERAL YEARS AGO, I READ Brian Aldiss's *Billion Year Spree*—his "true history of science fiction" from Mary Shelley to the early 1970s. I admire Aldiss tremendously, and I found his account of the genre's development entertaining and informative... but something bothered me, after I'd finished reading the book. Something was missing.

Billion Year Spree is terrific on the topic of science fiction from *Frankenstein* through the "scientific romances" of Verne, Poe, and Wells—and also terrific on science fiction's so-called Golden Age, the start of which sf exegetes date to John W. Campbell's 1937 assumption of the editorship of the magazine *Astounding*. However, regarding science fiction published between the beginning of the Golden Age and the end of the Verne-Poe-Wells "scientific romance" era, Aldiss (who rightly laments that Wells's 20th century fiction after, perhaps, 1904's *The Food of the Gods*, fails to recapture "that darkly beautiful quality of imagination, or that instinctive-seeming unity of construction, which lives in his early novels") has very little to say.

Aldiss seems to feel that authors of science fiction after Wells but before the Golden Age weren't very talented. He certainly doesn't think much of the literary skills of Hugo Gernsback, sometimes called the "Father of Science Fiction," who founded *Amazing Stories* in 1926 and coined the phrase "science fiction" while he was at it. He's right: Gernsback's story-telling abilities were as primitive as his ideas were advanced. But does that justify skipping over the 1904-33 era? (By my reckoning, Campbell and his cohort first began to develop their literate, analytical, socially conscious science fiction in reaction to the 1934 advent of the campy *Flash Gordon* comic strip, not to mention Hollywood's "sci-fi" blockbusters that sought to ape the success of 1933's *King Kong*. In other words, sf's Golden Age began before 1937; if I had to pick a year, I'd say 1934.) Is Aldiss's animus against that era due solely to style and quality? I suspect not.

Aldiss's book is hardly alone in sweeping pre-1934 science fiction under the rug. During the so-called Golden Age, which was given that moniker not after the fact, but *at the time*, as a way of signifying the end of science fiction's post-Wells Dark Age, Campbellians took pains to distinguish their own science fiction from everything that had been published in the genre (with the sole exception of

1932's *Brave New World*) since 1904. In his influential 1958 critique, *New Maps of Hell*, for example, Kingsley Amis noted that mature science fiction first established itself in the mid-1930s, "separating with a slowly increasing decisiveness from [immature] fantasy and space-opera." And in his introduction to a 1974 collection, *Before the Golden Age*, editor Isaac Asimov apologetically notes that although it certainly possessed an exuberant vigor, the pre-Golden Age science fiction he grew up reading "seems, to anyone who has experienced the Campbell Revolution, to be clumsy, primitive, naive."

We should be suspicious of this Cold War-era rhetoric of maturity! I'm reminded of Reinhold Niebuhr's pronunciamento, at a 1952 *Partisan Review* symposium, that the utopianism of the early 20th century ought to be regarded as "an adolescent embarrassment." Perhaps Golden Age science fiction's stars—Asimov, Robert Heinlein, Ray Bradbury, and so forth—were regarded as an improvement on their predecessors because in their stories utopian visions and schemes were treated with cynicism. Liberal and conservative anti-utopians who point out that pre-Cold War utopian narratives often demonstrate a naive and perhaps proto-totalitarian eagerness to force square pegs into round holes via thought control and coercion are not wrong. I wouldn't want to live in one of those utopias. However, I strongly agree with those who argue that the intellectual abandonment of utopianism since the 1930s has sapped our political options, and left us all in the helpless position of passive accomplices.

Sure, some 1904–33 science fiction—Gernsback, Edgar Rice Burroughs, and E.E. "Doc" Smith, for example—is indeed fantastical and primitive (though it's still fun to read today). But many other authors of that period—including Olaf Stapledon, William Hope Hodgson, Karel Čapek, Charlotte Perkins Gilman, and Yevgeny Zamyatin—gave us science fiction that was literate, analytical, socially conscious… and also utopian. Utopian in the sense that whatever their politics, Radium Age authors found in the newly named "science fiction" genre a fitting vehicle to express their faith, or at least their hope, that another world is possible. That worldview may have seemed embarrassingly adolescent from the late 1930s until, say, the fall of the Berlin Wall. But today it's an inspiring vision.

—*Joshua Glenn*
Cofounder,
HiLobrow.com & HiLoBooks
Boston, 2012

HiLoBooks
RADIUM AGE SCIENCE FICTION

2012

The Scarlet Plague
Jack London
Comment by Matthew Battles

With the Night Mail and "As Easy as A.B.C."
Rudyard Kipling
Comments by Matthew De Abaitua & Bruce Sterling

The Poison Belt
Arthur Conan Doyle
Comments by Joshua Glenn & Gordon Dahlquist

When the World Shook
H. Rider Haggard
Comment by James Parker

People of the Ruins
Edward Shanks

The Night Land
William Hope Hodgson
Comment by Erik Davis

Table of Contents

Thoughts About an Airship

Introduction by Matthew De Abaitua

IN 1870, THE PRUSSIAN ARMY laid siege to Paris, a city of Jules Verne modernity. This Paris harboured malfunctioning prototypes of the future—the *mitrailleuse* machine gun and *Le Plongeur* submarine—and aborted deranged technologies such as Jules Allix's long-distance communication system based on the telegraphic escargot fluid of "sympathetic snails," a fever dream of quantum entanglement. Hemmed in by the Prussian military, Parisians were forced to dine on rats or—if they were lucky—choice cuts from the exotic species in the city zoo.

The only way out of the siege was up. In the disused termini of the imprisoned city—the Gare Du Nord and Garde d'Orléans—lines of seamstresses manufactured hot air balloons to be launched from the Solferino Tower in Montmartre bearing military orders and American arms dealers. Stinking with gas and reliant upon a favourable weather forecast, the balloons flew in jagged haphazard fashion over enemy lines. Their flight was observed by two Prussian officers whose names would soon float above the world: Lieutenant Paul von Hindenburg and Captain Count Ferdinand von Zeppelin.

Four years later, the German Postmaster General Heinrich von Stephan gave a lecture on "World Mail and Air Travel." The postmaster reminded his audience of the Prussian siege of Paris and how over sixty balloons had escaped carrying mail. After reading an account of this lecture, Count Zeppelin turned to his diary and, under the heading "Thoughts About an Airship," set down his vision of the dirigible: it must have the dimensions of a big ship, be dynamically powered, and constructed of longitudinal girders and rings each of which would contain an individual gas cell or gasbag.

In a dirigible—from the French *diriger* (to steer)—the aeronaut steers through the wind. The technology for a steerable balloon had been invented at the same time as the first balloon flight of the *Mont-golfière* in 1783: gasbags or internal envelopes within the balloon in which air pressure could be increased or decreased without venting hydrogen, thereby controlling buoyancy and altitude over a prolonged duration. Additional propulsion was required, and could be provided by a screw or propellor as in a steam ship. But a steam engine was too heavy for air travel, and so the dirigible had to wait a hundred years for the invention of the lighter petrol combustion engine.

After retiring from the military at 52, Count Zeppelin turned his dream of an airship into a reality and flew the *LZ-1* on July 2 in 1900, powered by two Daimler petrol engines. The flight lasted eighteen minutes.

Advocates of the aeroplane argued with the believers in the balloon as to which method would prove to be the future of air travel. This argument is dramatised in Jules Verne's *Clipper of the Clouds* (1886) in which a balloon society is scandalised by the aeronaut Robur; he dismisses the dirigible and unveils his aeroplane, a "clipper" a hundred feet long and twelve feet wide with thirty seven masts each bearing two propellors, and powered by electricity: the faux science of the ship—that is, the dilithium crystals in its warp engines—are the acids and construction of accumulators that generated such currents, and all unpatented. The endurance of the airship as symbol of alternative history, a steampunk cliche, derives from the arguments dramatised in Verne's *Clipper of the Clouds*: aeroplanes or dirigibles, two time streams, two possible futures,

Flight was a symbol of fin de siècle futurity, a standard entry in predictions of what the twentieth century would hold. Verne's contemporary Albert Robida explores these prophecies in his novel *Vingtième Siècle* (1882) and in his illustrations of a future Paris. Robida painted airborne socialites docking on platforms to dine in restaurants in the sky and cavalry riding batwing rockets into battle. With the turn of the century, the playfulness of the balloon was challenged by the dirigible. If the *Montgolfière* represented the wandering aimless flight of whimsy, the Zeppelin fused imagination to the will to become an object feared and adored: the technological sublime.

In the First World War, the Zeppelin was deployed in the bombing of London. In a letter of 1915, D.H. Lawrence observes the bright golden finger of the airship as it destroys the old order and points the way toward what will replace it: "Then we saw the Zeppelin above us, just ahead, amid a gleaming of clouds: high up, like a bright golden finger, quite small, among a fragile incandescence of clouds. And underneath it were splashes of fire as the shells fired from the earth burst. Then there were flashes near the ground—and the shaking noise. It was like Milton—then there was war in heaven. But it was not angels. It was that small golden Zeppelin, like a long oval world, high up. It seemed as if the cosmic order were gone, as if there had come a new order, a new heaven above us: and as if the world in anger were trying to revoke it. Then the small, long-ovate luminary, the new world in the heavens, disappeared again... So it is the end—our world is gone."

The airship was an ideal of the new order and the means of achieving it. In H.G. Wells' *War In The Air* (1908), a German air fleet bombs New York. The war fleet consists of the "lineal descendants of the Zeppelin airship that flew over Lake Constance in 1906"; that is, the *LZ2*, which more closely resembled an inter-continental missile than the bosomy bloat of later craft. *War In The Air* depicts a dozen German airships destroying the American naval fleet from a height of two thousand feet before arriving in New York in late afternoon. The airships loom over the city in the same way that the enormous UFOs of *V*, *Independence Day* and *District 9* are suspended impossibly above the heads of the citizens. The apocalypse is preceded by weightless moments of delicious anticipation: "there the monsters hung, large and wonderful in the evening light, serenely regardless of the occasional rocket explosions and flashing shell-bursts in the lower air."

New York surrenders to the airships and then rebels: "In this manner the massacre of New York began," writes Wells. "She was the first of the great cities of the Scientific Age to suffer by the enormous powers and grotesque limitations of aerial warfare... it was impossible to subdue the city except by largely destroying it." Nation states unleash fleets of airships. World War begins. European civilisation is blown up and "within five years it was altogether disintegrated and destroyed." Written seven years prior to the beginning of the First World War, Wells' closing lines anticipate the way in which war can overtake a civilisation: "somebody somewhere ought to have stopped something."

Wells got his eschatological kicks in envisioning the collapse of nation states and their replacement by a new world order: "it is chaos or the United States of the World for mankind," he wrote. After the First World War, in an article for the *Atlantic Monthly*, he pressed his belief in a League of Nations: the technological contrivances of science would make war borderless and increasingly destructive and so a unification of world states, following the progressive direction of history, would prevent the apocalyptic conflicts of the future. The League of Nations failed largely because the United States ignored it. An alternative timeline can be discerned: in the midst of the First World War, Zeppelin commander Peter Strasser had sought permission to bomb New York to arrest the flow of supplies to the allies. Had Strasser's plan gone ahead, would it have been a Pearl Harbor moment to lead America into the League of Nations?

HiLoBooks

The two stories by Rudyard Kipling collected in this volume, *With the Night Mail: A Story of 2000 AD Together with Extracts from the Magazine in Which It Appeared*, first published in *McClure's Magazine* in 1905 and reprinted in volume form in *Actions and Reactions* (1909), and its sequel "As Easy as A.B.C.," first published in 1912 in *London* magazine, and collected in *A Diversity of Creatures* in 1917, depict the role of airships in a new world order and are founding works of science fiction, or scientific romance as it was then called.

With the Night Mail is a journalistic account of a run aboard an airship carrying the mail from London to Quebec. From his late teenage years to his mid-twenties, Kipling worked on newspapers in Lahore and Allahabad, and he uses newsprint conventions for verisimilitude: the report of the story is followed by various advertisements, notes and correspondence from the future world of 2000 AD.

In the story itself, Kipling uses spurious technical terms to cultivate the reader's credulity: terms such as *Fleury's Ray* and *colloid*—which appears to be a kind of cellulose transparent substance used instead of glass for the portholes of the airship. Contemporary anxieties concerning German manufacturing appear when an airship using "German compos in their thrust-blocks" suffers difficulties. British manufacturing is "a shining reproof to all low-grade German 'ruby' enamels, so-called 'boort' facings, and the dangerous and unsatisfactory alumina compounds which please dividend-hunting owners and turn skippers crazy."

Arnold Bennett described *With the Night Mail* as "a glittering essay in the sham technical." He complained that mechanics displaced psychological accuracy, a perennial literary criticism of science fiction (C.S. Lewis observed that Arthur C. Clarke's stories were "engineer stories"). Kipling, with his obsession for motor cars and anti-intellectualism, delighted in the mechanical. Unlike other writers with literary reputations who have utilised science fiction tropes, Kipling is more interested in the nuts and bolts of the future than any grand ideas. He utilises a wide practical vocabulary with nautical terms such as *caisson*—a watertight chamber—overlapping with technological neologisms, a stylistic tactic similar to that presented by Ridley Scott in *Alien*: a weathered blue-collar future in which people still had to go to work.

The night mail airship slips its mooring tower and lights out across Ireland, passing over Valentia Island, landing point of the early transatlantic telegraph wires that connected Britain to the New World. Navigation through the cloudscape is made possible by cloud breakers, powerful lights beamed up from the earth and coloured according to region (green for Ireland, inevitably). Kipling imagines the scene vividly: "He points to the pillars of light where the cloud-breakers bore through the cloud-floor. We see nothing of England's outlines: only a white pavement pierced in all directions by these manholes of variously coloured fire." A master of action, Kipling's scenes of airship destruction are exhilarating; a stricken airship is driven from the shipping lanes by dropping a sofa-sized pithing-iron through its hull: "The derelict's forehead is punched in, starred across, and rent diagonally. She falls stern first, our beam upon her; slides like a lost soul down that pitiless ladder of light, and the Atlantic takes her."

The height of the adventure is the navigation of a fierce storm. The pilot, in an inflatable suit, flies the airship by hand through a landscape of crackling electricity, St. Elmo's fire and charged Krypton vapours. Kipling's mystical meteorology is an alluring example of how in the early years of the century advances in scientific knowledge had not completed their separation from supernatural and religious modes of thought. For a Victorian gentlemen adjusting to Edwardian future shock, the telephone was on the same timeline as the spiritualist's knock on the table. Arthur Conan Doyle wrote of the rational observation of Sherlock Holmes while believing in fairies at the bottom of the garden. The Society of Psychical Research pursued poltergeists with the rigour of amateur archaeologists. The overlap between induction, Marconi, and spiritualism forms the basis of Kipling's short story "Wireless," in which a consumptive picks up on the signal of the poet John Keats, presumably across the ether so beloved of Victorian physicists. The categories are in the process of being defined. Pierre Teilhard de Chardin, the Jesuit priest whose mystical-scientific conception of the noösphere would go onto inspire the post-human movement, was thrilled by the play of the supernatural and the mechanical within Kipling's stories; "they make ships and locomotives speak, they make you feel with the eastern soul."

The back story of *With the Night Mail* concerns the semi-elected, semi-nominated body of a few score of persons of both sexes who control the planet: the Aeronautical Board of Control, or A.B.C., a technocracy with the motto of "Transport is Civilisation." "As Easy as A.B.C.," the sequel to *With the Night Mail*, is set sixty-five years later and explores the global governance of this supranational agency. The prospect of a World Government is as much a futuristic trope of the era as the airship, and was a political cause advanced by H.G. Wells' United States of the World and the League of Peace advocated by Theodore Roosevelt's Nobel acceptance speech in 1910. Roosevelt and Kipling were friends and the A.B.C. and the League of Peace stem from their hearty can-do masculinity. The rule of law is dictated by "the wise and strong," pugnacious types who despise cowards and bullies alike. In the words of Roosevelt, "No nation deserves to exist if it permits itself to lose the stern and virile virtues." The association of the tumescent dirigible with virile order is undeniable; to paraphrase Freud, sometimes a cigar is just a cigar but an airship is never merely an airship.

The future of the A.B.C. is neither degenerate nor especially virile. Technological advance has transformed the dirigibles of the *Night Mail* into craft that shoot up rocket-fashion "like the 'aeroplane' of our ancestors." In 2065, democracy is a disease belonging to a bygone age of crowds. There has been no media or news sheets for twenty-seven years as they infringe upon privacy, and privacy is the paramount virtue of the future. Mankind has spread apart on the face of the earth, its numbers controlled and falling. Crowds and the "people" are bogeymen. War is obsolete. The A.B.C. maintains a fleet to deal with outbursts of democratic sentiments, and one such mission forms the basis of the story.

Kipling's ambiguity toward this future is apparent: authority figures weep at the deployment of non-lethal light and sound weapons, so unaccustomed have they become to death. With everyone provisioned and cared for by a benign technocracy, the peaks and troughs of life's oscillation are trimmed. It is an era averse to risk and waning nations gladly give up self-determination to the A.B.C. This passive compliance with the supranational technocracy, long portrayed as evidence of Kipling's misanthropy, is prophetic of the current response of an exhausted debt-burdened Europe to financial crisis.

During the writing of these two stories, Kipling lived in the remote estate of Bateman's in East Sussex. The highpoint of Kiplingism was the 1890s when it was a vital force in the school days of H. G. Wells. By 1910, Kipling's reputation was eclipsed by the onset of modernism in Britain with Roger Fry's exhibition of Post-Impressionism. It was the year when everything changed, according to Virginia Woolf. As Edmund Wilson observes, Kipling was only forty-five at this time, yet he was "dropped out of modern literature" and became "the thick, dark and surly little man who had dug himself into Bateman's, Burwash, Sussex." It is appropriate that his future of

Rudyard Kipling's WITH THE NIGHT MAIL

2065 is a depopulated world obsessed with privacy, the three million citizens of London dispersed easily across outlying towns—the current population of London is more than twice that and is packed into a much smaller area.

The airships of the A.B.C enforce elite rule from a dispassionate vantage point in the clouds. Democracy came from the ground up, the mass enfranchisement of the man of the street. Kipling's stories are an anxious response to the advancing power of the crowd and indicative of his personal isolation.

The benign anti-democratic rule of Kipling's A.B.C. anticipate the direction of H.G. Wells and his followers in the 1930s. The journal of the H.G. Wells society, *Cosmopolis*, advanced the cause of world unity then merged with *The Plan*, the journal for the Federation of Progressive Societies and Individuals. The disparate groups of the left recognised the need to band together to resist the fascist agglomeration, an aggressive praxis that Wells described in a lecture as "liberal fascism." They stood for a planned economy, the rule of the intellectual, production for use rather than profit and resistance to the racial myths and discredited eugenics of Hitler. One clear distinction between liberal fascism and its Nazi enemy was that the airships of the progressive forces remained on the drawing board of the imagination.

1937. Mid-afternoon in Manhattan. The Luftschiff Zeppelin #129 drifts over the south side of the island, its long shadow passing over the nail bed of the New York skyline. With a swastika on its tail fins, the *Hindenburg* is the Nazi herald and possesses the weightless solidity of a dictator.

Four and half hours later, as the airship manoeuvres toward a mooring mast in a field in Lakehurst, New Jersey, a mushroom-shaped flower of flame bursts in front of its upper fin. The roaring advance of the fire peels back the outer skin of the bow to reveal the bulkhead, and for an instant, the exposed skeleton is intact. The gaseous interior of the airship blazes. The structure melts and collapses face first into the earth. On the ground, sailors run toward the burnt bones.

The blazing *Hindenburg* cauterises the timeline of the airship. One future is destroyed and another takes its place. The dirigible becomes a symbol of the hallucination of security of day-to-day life, a hallucination that may one day crumple to earth—in the words of H.G. Wells—"like an exploded bladder."

WITH THE NIGHT MAIL

AT NINE O'CLOCK OF A GUSTY WINTER NIGHT I stood on the lower stages of one of the G.P.O. outward mail towers. My purpose was a run to Quebec in "Postal Packet 162 or such other as may be appointed"; and the Postmaster-General himself countersigned the order. This talisman opened all doors, even those in the despatching-caisson at the foot of the tower, where they were delivering the sorted Continental mail. The bags lay packed close as herrings in the long gray under-bodies which our G.P.O. still calls "coaches." Five such coaches were filled as I watched, and were shot up the guides to be locked on to their waiting packets three hundred feet nearer the stars.

From the despatching-caisson I was conducted by a courteous and wonderfully learned official—Mr. L. L. Geary, Second Despatcher of the Western Route—to the Captains' Room (this wakes an echo of old romance), where the mail captains come on for their turn of duty. He introduces me to the Captain of "162"—Captain Purnall, and his relief, Captain Hodgson. The one is small and dark; the other large and red; but each has the brooding sheathed glance characteristic of eagles and aëronauts. You can see it in the pictures of our racing professionals, from L. V. Rautsch to little Ada Warrleigh—that fathomless abstraction of eyes habitually turned through naked space.

On the notice-board in the Captains' Room, the pulsing arrows of some twenty indicators register, degree by geographical degree, the progress of as many homeward-bound packets. The word "Cape" rises across the face of a dial; a gong strikes: the South African mid-weekly mail is in at the Highgate Receiving Towers. That is all. It reminds one comically of the traitorous little bell which in pigeon-fanciers' lofts notifies the return of a homer.

"Time for us to be on the move," says Captain Purnall, and we are shot up by the passenger-lift to the top of the despatch-towers. "Our coach will lock on when it is filled and the clerks are aboard." …

"No. 162" waits for us in Slip E of the topmost stage. The great curve of her back shines frostily under the lights, and some minute alteration of trim makes her rock a little in her holding-down slips.

Captain Purnall frowns and dives inside. Hissing softly, "162" comes to rest as level as a rule. From her North Atlantic Winter nose-cap (worn bright as diamond with boring through uncounted leagues of hail, snow, and ice) to the inset of her three built-out propeller-shafts is some two hundred and forty feet. Her extreme diameter, carried well forward, is thirty-seven. Contrast this with the nine hundred by ninety-five of any crack liner and you will realize the power that must drive a hull through all weathers at more than the emergency-speed of the "Cyclonic"!

The eye detects no joint in her skin plating save the sweeping hair-crack of the bow-rudder— Magniac's rudder that assured us the dominion of the unstable air and left its inventor penniless and half-blind. It is calculated to Castelli's "gullwing" curve. Raise a few feet of that all but invisible plate three-eighths of an inch and she will yaw five miles to port or starboard ere she is under control again. Give her full helm and she returns on her track like a whip-lash. Cant the whole forward—a touch on the wheel will suffice—and she sweeps at your good direction up or down. Open the complete circle and she presents to the air a mushroom-head that will bring her up all standing within a half mile.

"Yes," says Captain Hodgson, answering my thought, "Castelli thought he'd discovered the secret of controlling aëroplanes when he'd only found out how to steer dirigible balloons. Magniac invented his rudder to help war-boats ram each other; and war went out of fashion and Magniac he went out of his mind because he said he couldn't serve his country any more. I wonder if any of us ever know what we're really doing."

"If you want to see the coach locked you'd better go aboard. It's due now," says Mr. Geary. I enter through the door amidships. There is nothing here for display. The inner skin of the gas-tanks comes down to within a foot or two of my head and turns over just short of the turn of the bilges. Liners and yachts disguise their tanks with decoration, but the G.P.O. serves them raw under a lick of gray official paint. The inner skin shuts off fifty feet of the bow and as much of the stern, but the bow-bulkhead is recessed for the lift-shunting apparatus as the stern is pierced for the shaft-tunnels. The engine-room lies almost amidships. Forward of it, extending to the turn of the bow tanks, is an aperture—a bottomless hatch at present—into which our coach will be locked. One looks down over the coamings three hundred feet to the despatching-caisson whence voices boom upward. The light below is obscured to a sound of thunder, as our coach rises on its guides. It enlarges rapidly from a postage-stamp to a playing-card; to a punt and last a pontoon. The two clerks, its crew, do not even look up as it comes into place. The Quebec letters fly under their fingers and leap into the docketed racks, while both captains and Mr. Geary satisfy themselves that the coach is locked home. A clerk passes the waybill over the hatch-coaming. Captain Purnall thumb-marks and passes it to Mr. Geary. Receipt has been given and taken. "Pleasant run," says Mr. Geary, and disappears through the door which a foot-high pneumatic compressor locks after him.

"A-ah!" sighs the compressor released. Our holding-down clips part with a tang. We are clear.

Captain Hodgson opens the great colloid underbody-porthole through which I watch million-lighted London slide eastward as the gale gets hold of us. The first of the low winter clouds cuts off the well-known view and darkens Middlesex. On the south edge of it I can see a postal packet's light ploughing through the white fleece. For an instant she gleams like a star ere she drops toward the Highgate Receiving Towers. "The Bombay Mail," says Captain Hodgson, and looks at his watch. "She's forty minutes late."

"What's our level?" I ask.

"Four thousand. Aren't you coming up on the bridge?"

The bridge (let us ever bless the G.P.O. as a repository of ancientest tradition!) is represented by a view of Captain Hodgson's legs where he stands on the control platform that runs thwart-ships overhead. The bow colloid is unshuttered and Captain Purnall, one hand on the wheel, is feeling for a fair slant. The dial shows 4,300 feet.

"It's steep to-night," he mutters, as tier on tier of cloud drops under. "We generally pick up an easterly draught below three thousand at this time o' the year. I hate slathering through fluff."

"So does Van Cutsem. Look at him huntin' for a slant!" says Captain Hodgson. A fog-light breaks cloud a hundred fathoms below. The Antwerp Night Mail makes her signal and rises between two racing clouds far to port, her flanks blood-red in the glare of Sheerness Double Light. The gale will have us over the North Sea in half an hour, but Captain Purnall lets her go composedly— nosing to every point of the compass as she rises.

"Five thousand—six, six thousand eight hundred"—the dip-dial reads ere we find the easterly drift, heralded by a flurry of snow at the thousand-fathom level. Captain Purnall rings up the engines and keys down the governor on the switch before him. There is no sense in urging machinery when

Æolus himself gives you good knots for nothing. We are away in earnest now—our nose notched home on our chosen star. At this level the lower clouds are laid out all neatly combed by the dry fingers of the East. Below that again is the strong westerly blow through which we rose. Overhead, a film of southerly drifting mist draws a theatrical gauze across the firmament. The moonlight turns the lower strata to silver without a stain except where our shadow underruns us. Bristol and Cardiff Double Lights (those statelily inclined beams over Severnmouth) are dead ahead of us; for we keep the Southern Winter Route. Coventry Central, the pivot of the English system, stabs upward once in ten seconds its spear of diamond light to the north; and a point or two off our starboard bow The Leek, the great cloud-breaker of Saint David's Head, swings its unmistakable green beam twenty-five degrees each way. There must be half a mile of fluff over it in this weather, but it does not affect The Leek.

"Our planet's overlighted if anything," says Captain Purnall at the wheel, as Cardiff-Bristol slides under. "I remember the old days of common white verticals that 'ud show two or three thousand feet up in a mist, if you knew where to look for 'em. In really fluffy weather they might as well have been under your hat. One could get lost coming home then, an' have some fun. Now, it's like driving down Piccadilly."

He points to the pillars of light where the cloud-breakers bore through the cloud-floor. We see nothing of England's outlines: only a white pavement pierced in all directions by these manholes of variously coloured fire—Holy Island's white and red—St. Bee's interrupted white, and so on as far as the eye can reach. Blessed be Sargent, Ahrens, and the Dubois brothers, who invented the cloud-breakers of the world whereby we travel in security!

"Are you going to lift for The Shamrock?" asks Captain Hodgson. Cork Light (green, fixed) enlarges as we rush to it. Captain Purnall nods. There is heavy traffic hereabouts—the cloud-bank beneath us is streaked with running fissures of flame where the Atlantic boats are hurrying Londonward just clear of the fluff. Mail-packets are supposed, under the Conference rules, to have the five-thousand-foot lanes to themselves, but the foreigner in a hurry is apt to take liberties with English air. "No. 162" lifts to a long-drawn wail of the breeze in the fore-flange of the rudder and we make Valencia (white, green, white) at a safe 7,000 feet, dipping our beam to an incoming Washington packet.

There is no cloud on the Atlantic, and faint

streaks of cream round Dingle Bay show where the driven seas hammer the coast. A big S.A.T.A. liner (*Société Anonyme des Transports Aëriens*) is diving and lifting half a mile below us in search of some break in the solid west wind. Lower still lies a disabled Dane: she is telling the liner all about it in International. Our General Communication dial has caught her talk and begins to eavesdrop. Captain Hodgson makes a motion to shut it off but checks himself. "Perhaps you'd like to listen," he says.

"'Argol' of St. Thomas," the Dane whimpers. "Report owners three starboard shaft collar-bearings fused. Can make Flores as we are, but impossible further. Shall we buy spares at Fayal?"

The liner acknowledges and recommends inverting the bearings. The "Argol" answers that she has already done so without effect, and begins to relieve her mind about cheap German enamels for collar-bearings. The Frenchman assents cordially, cries "*Courage, mon ami,*" and switches off.

Their lights sink under the curve of the ocean.

"That's one of Lundt & Bleamers's boats," says Captain Hodgson. "Serves 'em right for putting German compos in their thrust-blocks. *She* won't be in Fayal to-night! By the way, wouldn't you like to look round the engine-room?"

I have been waiting eagerly for this invitation and I follow Captain Hodgson from the control-platform, stooping low to avoid the bulge of the tanks. We know that Fleury's gas can lift anything, as the world-famous trials of '89 showed, but its almost indefinite powers of expansion necessitate vast tank room. Even in this thin air the lift-shunts are busy taking out one-third of its normal lift, and still "162" must be checked by an occasional downdraw of the rudder or our flight would become a climb to the stars. Captain Purnall prefers an overlifted to an underlifted ship; but no two captains trim ship alike. "When *I* take the bridge," says Captain Hodgson, "you'll see me shunt forty per cent. of the lift out of the gas and run her on the upper rudder. With a swoop upwards instead of a swoop downwards, *as* you say. Either way will do. It's only habit. Watch our dip-dial! Tim fetches her down once every thirty knots as regularly as breathing."

So is it shown on the dip-dial. For five or six minutes the arrow creeps from 6,700 to 7,300. There is the faint "szgee" of the rudder, and back slides the arrow to 6,500 on a falling slant of ten or fifteen knots.

"In heavy weather you jockey her with the screws as well," says Captain Hodgson, and, unclipping the jointed bar which divides the engine-room from the bare deck, he leads me on to the floor.

Here we find Fleury's Paradox of the Bulkheaded Vacuum—which we accept now without thought—literally in full blast. The three engines are H.T. &. T. assisted-vacuo Fleury turbines running from 3,000 to the Limit—that is to say, up to the point when the blades make the air "bell"— cut out a vacuum for themselves precisely as over-driven marine propellers used to do. "162's" Limit is low on account of the small size of her nine screws, which, though handier than the old colloid Thelussons, "bell" sooner. The midships engine, generally used as a reinforce, is not running; so the port and starboard turbine vacuum-chambers draw direct into the return-mains.

The turbines whistle reflectively. From the low-arched expansion-tanks on either side the valves descend pillarwise to the turbine-chests, and thence the obedient gas whirls through the spirals of blades with a force that would whip the teeth out of a power-saw. Behind, is its own pressure held in leash or spurred on by the lift-shunts; before it, the vacuum where Fleury's Ray dances in violet-green bands and whirled turbillions of flame. The jointed U-tubes of the vacuum-chamber are pressure-tempered colloid (no glass would endure the strain for an instant) and a junior engineer with tinted spectacles watches the Ray intently. It is the very heart of the machine—a mystery to this day. Even Fleury who begat it and, unlike Magniac, died a multi-millionaire, could not explain how the restless little imp shuddering in the U-tube can, in the fractional fraction of a second, strike the furious blast of gas into a chill grayish-green liquid that drains (you can hear it trickle) from the far end of the vacuum through the eduction-pipes and the mains back to the bilges. Here it returns to its gaseous, one had almost written sagacious, state and climbs to work afresh. Bilge-tank, upper tank, dorsal-tank, expansion-chamber, vacuum, main-return (as a liquid), and bilge-tank once more is the ordained cycle. Fleury's Ray sees to that; and the engineer with the tinted spectacles sees to Fleury's Ray. If a speck of oil, if even the natural grease of the human finger touch the hooded terminals Fleury's Ray will wink and disappear and must be laboriously built up again. This means half a day's work for all hands and an expense of one hundred and seventy-odd pounds to the G.P.O. for radium-salts and such trifles.

"Now look at our thrust-collars. You won't find much German compo there. Full-jewelled, you see," says Captain Hodgson as the engineer shunts open the top of a cap. Our shaft-bearings are C.M.C. (Commercial Minerals Company) stones, ground with as much care as the lens of a telescope. They cost £37 apiece. So far we have not arrived at their term of life. These bearings came from "No. 97," which took them over from the old "Dominion of Light," which had them out of the wreck of the "Perseus" aëroplane in the years when men still flew linen kites over thorium engines!

They are a shining reproof to all low-grade German "ruby" enamels, so-called "boort" facings, and the dangerous and unsatisfactory alumina compounds which please dividend-hunting owners and turn skippers crazy.

The rudder-gear and the gas lift-shunt, seated side by side under the engine-room dials, are the only machines in visible motion. The former sighs from time to time as the oil plunger rises and falls half an inch. The latter, cased and guarded like the U-tube aft, exhibits another Fleury Ray, but inverted and more green than violet. Its function is to shunt the lift out of the gas, and this it will do without watching. That is all! A tiny pump-rod wheezing and whining to itself beside a sputtering green lamp. A hundred and fifty feet aft down the flat-topped tunnel of the tanks a violet light, restless and irresolute. Between the two, three white-painted turbine-trunks, like eel-baskets laid on their side, accentuate the empty perspectives. You can hear the trickle of the liquefied gas flowing from the vacuum into the bilge-tanks and the soft *gluck-glock* of gas-locks closing as Captain Purnall brings "162" down by the head. The hum of the turbines and the boom of the air on our skin is no more than a cotton-wool wrapping to the universal stillness. And we are running an eighteen-second mile.

I peer from the fore end of the engine-room over the hatch-coamings into the coach. The mail-clerks are sorting the Winnipeg, Calgary, and Medicine Hat bags: but there is a pack of cards ready on the table.

Suddenly a bell thrills; the engineers run to the turbine-valves and stand by; but the spectacled slave of the Ray in the U-tube never lifts his head. He must watch where he is. We are hard-braked and going astern; there is language from the control-platform.

"Tim's sparking badly about something," says the unruffled Captain Hodgson. "Let's look."

Captain Purnall is not the suave man we left half an hour since, but the embodied authority of the G.P.O. Ahead of us floats an ancient, aluminum-patched, twin-screw tramp of the dingiest, with no more right to the 5,000 foot lane than has a horse-cart to a modern town. She carries an obsolete "barbette" conning-tower—a six-foot affair with railed platform forward—and our warning beam plays on the top of it as a policeman's lantern flashes on the area sneak. Like a sneak-thief, too, emerges a shock-headed navigator in his shirt-sleeves. Captain Purnall wrenches open the colloid to talk with him man to man. There are times when Science does not satisfy.

"What under the stars are you doing here, you sky-scraping chimney-sweep?" he shouts as we two drift side by side. "Do you know this is a Mail-lane? You call yourself a sailor, sir? You ain't fit to peddle toy balloons to an Esquimaux. Your name and number! Report and get down, and be——!"

"I've been blown up once," the shock-headed man cries, hoarsely, as a dog barking. "I don't care two flips of a contact for anything *you* can do, Postey."

"Don't you, sir? But I'll make you care. I'll have you towed stern first to Disko and broke up. You can't recover insurance if you're broke for obstruction. Do you understand *that*?"

Then the stranger bellows: "Look at my propellers! There's been a wulli-wa down under that has knocked us into umbrella-frames! We've been blown up about forty thousand feet! We're all one conjuror's watch inside! My mate's arm's broke; my engineer's head's cut open; my Ray went out when the engines smashed; and… and… for pity's sake give me my height, Captain! We doubt we're dropping."

"Six thousand eight hundred. Can you hold it?" Captain Purnall overlooks all insults, and leans half out of the colloid, staring and snuffing. The stranger leaks pungently.

"We ought to blow into St. John's with luck. We're trying to plug the fore-tank now, but she's simply whistling it away," her captain wails.

"She's sinking like a log," says Captain Purnall in an undertone. "Call up the Banks Mark Boat, George." Our dip-dial shows that we, keeping abreast the tramp, have dropped five hundred feet the last few minutes.

Captain Purnall presses a switch and our signal beam begins to swing through the night, twizzling spokes of light across infinity.

"That'll fetch something," he says, while Captain Hodgson watches the General Communicator. He has called up the North Banks Mark Boat, a few hundred miles west, and is reporting the case.

"I'll stand by you," Captain Purnall roars to the lone figure on the conning-tower.

"Is it as bad as that?" comes the answer. "She isn't insured, she's mine."

"Might have guessed as much," mutters Hodgson. "Owner's risk is the worst risk of all!"

"Can't I fetch St. John's—not even with this breeze?" the voice quavers.

"Stand by to abandon ship. Haven't you *any* lift

in you, fore or aft?"

"Nothing but the midship tanks and they're none too tight. You see, my Ray gave out and—" he coughs in the reek of the escaping gas.

"You poor devil!" This does not reach our friend. "What does the Mark Boat say, George?"

"Wants to know if there's any danger to traffic. Says she's in a bit of weather herself and can't quit station. I've turned in a General Call, so even if they don't see our beam some one's bound to help—or else we must. Shall I clear our slings. Hold on! Here we are! A Planet liner, too! She'll be up in a tick!"

"Tell her to have her slings ready," cries his brother captain. "There won't be much time to spare.... Tie up your mate," he roars to the tramp.

"My mate's all right. It's my engineer. He's gone crazy."

"Shunt the lift out of him with a spanner. Hurry!"

"But I can make St. John's if you'll stand by."

"You'll make the deep, wet Atlantic in twenty minutes. You're less than fifty-eight hundred now. Get your papers."

A Planet liner, east bound, heaves up in a superb spiral and takes the air of us humming. Her underbody colloid is open and her transporter-slings hang down like tentacles. We shut off our beam as she adjusts herself—steering to a hair—over the tramp's conning-tower. The mate comes up, his arm strapped to his side, and stumbles into the cradle. A man with a ghastly scarlet head follows, shouting that he must go back and build up his Ray. The mate assures him that he will find a nice new Ray all ready in the liner's engine-room. The bandaged head goes up wagging excitedly. A youth and a woman follow. The liner cheers hollowly above us, and we see the passengers' faces at the saloon colloid.

"That's a good girl. What's the fool waiting for now?" says Captain Purnall.

The skipper comes up, still appealing to us to stand by and see him fetch St. John's. He dives below and returns—at which we little human beings in the void cheer louder than ever—with the ship's kitten. Up fly the liner's hissing slings; her underbody crashes home and she hurtles away again. The dial shows less than 3,000 feet.

The Mark Boat signals we must attend to the derelict, now whistling her death song, as she falls beneath us in long sick zigzags.

"Keep our beam on her and send out a General Warning," says Captain Purnall, following her down.

There is no need. Not a liner in air but knows the meaning of that vertical beam and gives us and our quarry a wide berth.

"But she'll drown in the water, won't she?" I ask.

"Not always," is his answer. "I've known a derelict up-end and sift her engines out of herself and flicker round the Lower Lanes for three weeks on her forward tanks only. We'll run no risks. Pith her, George, and look sharp. There's weather ahead."

Captain Hodgson opens the underbody colloid, swings the heavy pithing-iron out of its rack which in liners is generally cased as a settee, and at two hundred feet releases the catch. We hear the whir of the crescent-shaped arms opening as they descend. The derelict's forehead is punched in, starred across, and rent diagonally. She falls stern first, our beam upon her; slides like a lost soul down that pitiless ladder of light, and the Atlantic takes her.

"A filthy business," says Hodgson. "I wonder what it must have been like in the old days."

The thought had crossed my mind too. What if that wavering carcass had been filled with International-speaking men of all the Internationalities, each one of them taught (*that* is the horror of it!) that after death he would very possibly go forever to unspeakable torment?

And not half a century since, we (one knows now that we are only our fathers re-enlarged upon the earth), *we*, I say, ripped and rammed and pithed to admiration.

Here Tim, from the control-platform, shouts that we are to get into our inflators and to bring him his at once.

We hurry into the heavy rubber suits—and the engineers are already dressed—and inflate at the air-pump taps. G.P.O. inflators are thrice as thick as a racing man's "flickers," and chafe abominably under the armpits. George takes the wheel until Tim has blown himself up to the extreme of rotundity. If you kicked him off the c.p. to the deck he would bounce back. But it is "162" that will do the kicking.

"The Mark Boat's mad—stark ravin' crazy," he snorts, returning to command. "She says there's a bad blow-out ahead and wants me to pull over to Greenland. I'll see her pithed first! We wasted an hour and a quarter over that dead duck down under, and now I'm expected to go rubbin' my back all round the Pole. What does she think a postal packet's made of? Gummed silk? Tell her we're coming on straight, George."

George buckles him into the Frame and switches on the Direct Control. Now under Tim's left toe lies the port-engine Accelerator; under his left heel the Reverse, and so with the other foot. The lift-shunt stops stand out on the rim of the steering-wheel where the fingers of his left hand can play on them. At his right hand is the midships engine lever ready to be thrown into gear at a moment's notice. He leans forward in his belt, eyes glued to the colloid, and one ear cocked toward the General Communicator. Henceforth he is the strength and direction of "162," through whatever may befall.

The Banks Mark Boat is reeling out pages of A.B.C. Directions to the traffic at large. We are to secure all "loose objects"; hood up our Fleury Rays; and "on no account to attempt to clear snow from our conning-towers till the weather abates." Under-powered craft, we are told, can ascend to the limit of their lift, mail-packets to look out for them accordingly; the lower lanes westward are pitting very badly, "with frequent blow-outs, vortices, laterals, etc."

Still the clear dark holds up unblemished. The only warning is the electric skin-tension (I feel as though I were a lace-maker's pillow) and an irritability which the gibbering of the General Communicator increases almost to hysteria.

We have made eight thousand feet since we pithed the tramp and our turbines are giving us an honest two hundred and ten knots.

Very far to the west an elongated blur of red, low down, shows us the North Banks Mark Boat.

There are specks of fire round her rising and falling—bewildered planets about an unstable sun—helpless shipping hanging on to her light for company's sake. No wonder she could not quit station.

She warns us to look out for the backwash of the bad vortex in which (her beam shows it) she is even now reeling.

The pits of gloom about us begin to fill with very faintly luminous films—wreathing and uneasy shapes. One forms itself into a globe of pale flame that waits shivering with eagerness till we sweep by. It leaps monstrously across the blackness, alights on the precise tip of our nose, pirouettes there an instant, and swings off. Our roaring bow sinks as though that light were lead—sinks and recovers to lurch and stumble again beneath the next blow-out. Tim's fingers on the lift-shunt strike chords of numbers—1:4:7:—2:4:6:—7:5:3, and so on; for he is running by his tanks only, lifting or lowering her against the uneasy air. All three engines are at work, for the sooner we have skated over this thin ice the better. Higher we dare not go. The whole upper vault is charged with pale krypton vapours, which our skin friction may excite to unholy manifestations. Between the upper and the lower levels—5,000, and 7,000, hints the Mark Boat—we may perhaps bolt through if.... Our bow clothes itself in blue flame and falls like a sword. No human skill can keep pace with the changing tensions. A vortex has us by the beak and we dive down a two-thousand-foot slant at an angle (the dip-dial and my bouncing body record it) of thirty-five. Our turbines scream shrilly; the propellers cannot bite on the thin air; Tim shunts the lift out of five tanks at once and by sheer weight drives her bulletwise through the maelstrom till she cushions with a jar on an up-gust, three thousand feet below.

"*Now* we've done it," says George in my ear. "Our skin-friction that last slide, has played Old Harry with the tensions! Look out for laterals, Tim, she'll want some holding."

"I've got her," is the answer. "Come *up*, old woman."

She comes up nobly, but the laterals buffet her left and right like the pinions of angry angels. She is jolted off her course in four ways at once, and cuffed into place again, only to be swung aside and dropped into a new chaos. We are never without a corposant grinning on our bows or rolling head over heels from nose to midships, and to the crackle of electricity around and within us is added once or twice the rattle of hail—hail that will never fall on any sea. Slow we must or we may break our back, pitch-poling.

"Air's a perfectly elastic fluid," roars George

41

above the tumult. "About as elastic as a head sea off the Fastnet, aint it?"

He is less than just to the good element. If one intrudes on the Heavens when they are balancing their volt-accounts; if one disturbs the High Gods' market-rates by hurling steel hulls at ninety knots across tremblingly adjusted electric tensions, one must not complain of any rudeness in the reception. Tim met it with an unmoved countenance, one corner of his under lip caught up on a tooth, his eyes fleeting into the blackness twenty miles ahead, and the fierce sparks flying from his knuckles at every turn of the hand. Now and again he shook his head to clear the sweat trickling from his eyebrows, and it was then that George, watching his chance, would slide down the life-rail and swab his face quickly with a big red handkerchief. I never imagined that a human being could so continuously labour and so collectedly think as did Tim through that Hell's half hour when the flurry was at its worst. We were dragged hither and yon by warm or frozen suctions, belched up on the tops of wulli-was, spun down by vortices and clubbed aside by laterals under a dizzying rush of stars in the company of a drunken moon. I heard the rushing click of the midship-engine-lever sliding in and out, the low growl of the lift-shunts, and, louder than the yelling winds without, the scream of the bow-rudder gouging into any lull that promised hold for an instant. At last we began to claw up on a cant, bow-rudder and port-propeller together; only the nicest balancing of tanks saved us from spinning like the rifle-bullet of the old days.

"We've got to hitch to windward of that Mark Boat somehow," George cried.

"There's no windward," I protested feebly, where I swung shackled to a stanchion. "How can there be?"

He laughed—as we pitched into a thousand foot blow-out—that red man laughed beneath his inflated hood!

"Look!" he said. "We must clear those refugees with a high lift."

The Mark Boat was below and a little to the sou'west of us, fluctuating in the centre of her distraught galaxy. The air was thick with moving lights at every level. I take it most of them were trying to lie head to wind but, not being hydras, they failed. An under-tanked Moghrabi boat had risen to the limit of her lift and, finding no improvement, had dropped a couple of thousand. There she met a superb wulli-wa and was blown up spinning like a dead leaf. Instead of shutting off she went astern and, naturally, rebounded as from a wall almost into the Mark Boat, whose language (our G.C. took it in) was humanly simple.

"If they'd only ride it out quietly it 'ud be better," said George in a calm, as we climbed like a bat above them all. "But some skippers *will* navigate without enough lift. What does that Tad-boat think she is doing, Tim?"

"Playin' kiss in the ring," was Tim's unmoved reply. A Trans-Asiatic Direct liner had found a smooth and butted into it full power. But there was a vortex at the tail of that smooth, so the T.A.D. was flipped out like a pea from off a fingernail, braking madly as she fled down and all but over-ending.

"Now I hope she's satisfied," said Tim. "I'm glad I'm not a Mark Boat… Do I want help?" The C.G. dial had caught his ear. "George, you may tell that gentleman with my love—love, remember, George—that I do not want help. Who *is* the officious sardine-tin?"

"A Rimouski drogher on the lookout for a tow."

"Very kind of the Rimouski drogher. This postal packet isn't being towed at present."

"Those droghers will go anywhere on a chance of salvage," George explained. "We call 'em kittiwakes."

A long-beaked, bright steel ninety-footer floated at ease for one instant within hail of us, her slings coiled ready for rescues, and a single hand in her open tower. He was smoking. Surrendered to the insurrection of the airs through which we tore our way, he lay in absolute peace. I saw the smoke of his pipe ascend untroubled ere his boat dropped, it seemed, like a stone in a well.

We had just cleared the Mark Boat and her disorderly neighbours when the storm ended as suddenly as it had begun. A shooting-star to northward filled the sky with the green blink of a meteorite dissipating itself in our atmosphere.

Said George: "That may iron out all the tensions." Even as he spoke, the conflicting winds came to rest; the levels filled; the laterals died out in long easy swells; the airways were smoothed before us. In less than three minutes the covey round the Mark Boat had shipped their power-lights and whirred away upon their businesses.

"What's happened?" I gasped. The nerve-storm within and the volt-tingle without had passed: my inflators weighed like lead.

"God, He knows!" said Captain George, soberly. "That old shooting-star's skin-friction has discharged the different levels. I've seen it happen before. Phew! What a relief!"

We dropped from ten to six thousand and got rid of our clammy suits. Tim shut off and stepped out of the Frame. The Mark Boat was coming up behind us. He opened the colloid in that heavenly stillness and mopped his face.

"Hello, Williams!" he cried. "A degree or two out o' station, ain't you?"

"May be," was the answer from the Mark Boat. "I've had some company this evening."

"So I noticed. Wasn't that quite a little draught?"

"I warned you. Why didn't you pull out round by Disko? The east-bound packets have."

"Me? Not till I'm running a Polar consumptives' Sanatorium boat. I was squinting through a colloid before you were out of your cradle, my son."

"I'd be the last man to deny it," the captain of the Mark Boat replies softly. "The way you handled her just now—I'm a pretty fair judge of traffic in a volt-flurry—it was a thousand revolutions beyond anything even *I*'ve ever seen."

Tim's back supples visibly to this oiling. Captain George on the c.p. winks and points to the portrait of a singularly attractive maiden pinned up on Tim's telescope-bracket above the steering-wheel.

I see. Wholly and entirely do I see!

There is some talk overhead of "coming round to tea on Friday," a brief report of the derelict's fate, and Tim volunteers as he descends: "For an A.B.C. man young Williams is less of a high-tension fool than some. . . Were you thinking of taking her on, George? Then I'll just have a look

46

round that port-thrust—seems to me it's a trifle warm—and we'll jog along."

The Mark Boat hums off joyously and hangs herself up in her appointed eyrie. Here she will stay, a shutterless observatory; a life-boat station; a salvage tug; a court of ultimate appeal-cum-meteorological bureau for three hundred miles in all directions, till Wednesday next when her relief slides across the stars to take her buffeted place. Her black hull, double conning-tower, and ever-ready slings represent all that remains to the planet of that odd old word authority. She is responsible only to the Aërial Board of Control—the A.B.C. of which Tim speaks so flippantly. But that semi-elected, semi-nominated body of a few score persons of both sexes, controls this planet. "Transportation is Civilization," our motto runs. Theoretically, we do what we please so long as we do not interfere with the traffic and *all it implies*. Practically, the A.B.C. confirms or annuls all international arrangements and, to judge from its last report, finds our tolerant, humorous, lazy little planet only too ready to shift the whole burden of private administration on its shoulders.

I discuss this with Tim, sipping maté on the c.p. while George fans her along over the white blur of the Banks in beautiful upward curves of fifty miles each. The dip-dial translates them on the tape in flowing freehand.

Tim gathers up a skein of it and surveys the last few feet, which record "162's" path through the volt-flurry.

"I haven't had a fever-chart like this to show up in five years," he says ruefully.

A postal packet's dip-dial records every yard of every run. The tapes then go to the A.B.C., which collates and makes composite photographs of them for the instruction of captains. Tim studies his irrevocable past, shaking his head.

"Hello! Here's a fifteen-hundred-foot drop at eighty-five degrees! We must have been standing on our heads then, George."

"You don't say so," George answers. "I fancied I noticed it at the time."

George may not have Captain Purnall's catlike swiftness, but he is all an artist to the tips of the broad fingers that play on the shunt-stops. The delicious flight-curves come away on the tape with never a waver. The Mark Boat's vertical spindle of light lies down to eastward, setting in the face of the following stars. Westward, where no planet should rise, the triple verticals of Trinity Bay (we keep still to the Southern route) make a low-lifting haze. We seem the only thing at rest under all the heavens; floating at ease till the earth's revolution shall turn up our landing-towers.

And minute by minute our silent clock gives us a sixteen-second mile.

"Some fine night," says Tim. "We'll be even with that clock's Master."

"He's coming now," says George, over his shoulder. "I'm chasing the night west."

The stars ahead dim no more than if a film of mist had been drawn under unobserved, but the deep air-boom on our skin changes to a joyful shout.

"The dawn-gust," says Tim. "It'll go on to meet the Sun. Look! Look! There's the dark being crammed back over our bow! Come to the after-colloid. I'll show you something."

The engine-room is hot and stuffy; the clerks in the coach are asleep, and the Slave of the Ray is near to follow them. Tim slides open the aft colloid and reveals the curve of the world—the ocean's deepest purple—edged with fuming and intolerable gold. Then the Sun rises and through the colloid strikes out our lamps. Tim scowls in his face.

"Squirrels in a cage," he mutters. "That's all we are. Squirrels in a cage! He's going twice as fast as us. Just you wait a few years, my shining friend and we'll take steps that will amaze you. *We'll* Joshua you!"

Yes, that is our dream: to turn all earth into the

Vale of Ajalon at our pleasure. So far, we can drag out the dawn to twice its normal length in these latitudes. But some day—even on the Equator—we shall hold the Sun level in his full stride.

Now we look down on a sea thronged with heavy traffic. A big submersible breaks water suddenly. Another and another follow with a swash and a suck and a savage bubbling of relieved pressures. The deep-sea freighters are rising to lung up after the long night, and the leisurely ocean is all patterned with peacock's eyes of foam.

"We'll lung up, too," says Tim, and when we return to the c.p. George shuts off, the colloids are opened, and the fresh air sweeps her out. There is no hurry. The old contracts (they will be revised at the end of the year) allow twelve hours for a run which any packet can put behind her in ten. So we breakfast in the arms of an easterly slant which pushes us along at a languid twenty.

To enjoy life, and tobacco, begin both on a sunny morning half a mile or so above the dappled Atlantic cloud-belts and after a volt-flurry which has cleared and tempered your nerves. While we discussed the thickening traffic with the superiority that comes of having a high level reserved to ourselves, we heard (and I for the first time) the morning hymn on a Hospital boat.

She was cloaked by a skein of ravelled fluff beneath us and we caught the chant before she rose into the sunlight. "*Oh, ye Winds of God,*" sang the unseen voices: "*bless ye the Lord! Praise Him and magnify Him forever!*"

We slid off our caps and joined in. When our shadow fell across her great open platforms they looked up and stretched out their hands neighbourly while they sang. We could see the doctors and the nurses and the white-button-like faces of the cot-patients. She passed slowly beneath us, heading northward, her hull, wet with the dews of the night, all ablaze in the sunshine. So took she the shadow of a cloud and vanished, her song continuing. *Oh, ye holy and humble men of heart, bless ye the Lord! Praise Him and magnify Him forever.*

"She's a public lunger or she wouldn't have been singing the *Benedicite*; and she's a Greenlander or she wouldn't have snow-blinds over her colloids," said George at last. "She'll be bound for Frederikshavn or one of the Glacier sanatoriums for a month. If she was an accident ward she'd be hung up at the eight-thousand-foot level. Yes—consumptives."

"Funny how the new things are the old things. I've read in books," Tim answered, "that savages used to haul their sick and wounded up to the tops of hills because microbes were fewer there.

We hoist 'em into sterilized air for a while. Same idea. How much do the doctors say we've added to the average life of a man?"

"Thirty years," says George with a twinkle in his eye. "Are we going to spend 'em all up here, Tim?"

"Flap along, then. Flap along. Who's hindering?" the senior captain laughed, as we went in.

We held a good lift to clear the coastwise and Continental shipping; and we had need of it. Though our route is in no sense a populated one, there is a steady trickle of traffic this way along. We met Hudson Bay furriers out of the Great Preserve, hurrying to make their departure from Bonavista with sable and black fox for the insatiable markets. We over-crossed Keewatin liners, small and cramped; but their captains, who see no land between Trepassy and Blanco, know what gold they bring back from West Africa. Trans-Asiatic Directs, we met, soberly ringing the world round the Fiftieth Meridian at an honest seventy knots; and white-painted Ackroyd & Hunt fruiters out of the south fled beneath us, their ventilated hulls whistling like Chinese kites. Their market is in the North among the northern sanatoria where you can smell their grapefruit and bananas across the cold snows. Argentine beef boats we sighted too, of enormous capacity and unlovely outline. They, too, feed the northern health stations in ice-bound ports where submersibles dare not rise.

Yellow-bellied ore-flats and Ungava petrol-tanks punted down leisurely out of the north like strings of unfrightened wild duck. It does not pay to "fly" minerals and oil a mile farther than is necessary; but the risks of transhipping to submersibles in the ice-pack off Nain or Hebron are so great that these heavy freighters fly down to Halifax direct, and scent the air as they go. They are the biggest tramps aloft except the Athabasca grain-tubs. But these last, now that the wheat is moved, are busy, over the world's shoulder, timber-lifting in Siberia.

We held to the St. Lawrence (it is astonishing how the old water-ways still pull us children of the air), and followed his broad line of black between its drifting ice blocks, all down the Park that the wisdom of our fathers—but every one knows the Quebec run.

We dropped to the Heights Receiving Towers twenty minutes ahead of time and there hung at ease till the Yokohama Intermediate Packet could pull out and give us our proper slip. It was curious to watch the action of the holding-down clips all along the frosty river front as the boats cleared or came to rest. A big Hamburger was leaving Pont Levis and her crew, unshipping the platform railings, began to sing "Elsinore"—the oldest of our chanteys. You know it of course:

Mother Rugen's tea-house on the Baltic—

Forty couple waltzing on the floor!

And you can watch my Ray,

For I must go away

And dance with Ella Sweyn at Elsinore!

Then, while they sweated home the covering-plates:

Nor-Nor-Nor-Nor-

West from Sourabaya to the Baltic—

Ninety knot an hour to the Skaw!

Mother Rugen's tea-house on the Baltic

And a dance with Ella Sweyn at Elsinore!

The clips parted with a gesture of indignant dismissal, as though Quebec, glittering under her snows, were casting out these light and unworthy lovers. Our signal came from the Heights. Tim turned and floated up, but surely then it was with passionate appeal that the great tower arms flung open—or did I think so because on the upper staging a little hooded figure also opened her arms wide towards her father?

*   *   *

In ten seconds the coach with its clerks clashed down to the receiving-caisson; the hostlers displaced the engineers at the idle turbines, and Tim, prouder of this than all, introduced me to the maiden of the photograph on the shelf. "And by the way," said he to her, stepping forth in sunshine under the hat of civil life, "I saw young Williams in the Mark Boat. I've asked him to tea on Friday."

AERIAL BOARD OF CONTROL BULLETIN

Lights

No changes in English Inland lights for week ending Dec. 18.

PLANETARY COASTAL LIGHTS. Week ending Dec. 18. Verde inclined guide-light changes from 1st proximo to triple flash—green white green—in place of occulting red as heretofore. The warning light for Harmattan winds will be continuous vertical glare (white) on all oases of trans-Saharan N.E. by E. Main Routes.

INVERCARGIL (N.Z.)—From 1st prox.: extreme southerly light (double red) will exhibit white beam inclined 45 degrees on approach of Southerly Buster. Traffic flies high off this coast between April and October.

TABLE BAY—Devil's Peak Glare removed to Simonsberg. Traffic making Table Mountain coastwise keep all lights from Three Anchor Bay at least five shipping hundred feet under, and do not round to till beyond E. shoulder Devil's Peak.

SANDHEADS LIGHT—Green triple vertical marks new private landing-stage for Bay and Burma traffic only.

SNAEFELL JOKUL—White occulting light withdrawn for winter.

PATAGONIA—No summer light south C. Pilar. This includes Staten Island and Port Stanley.

C. NAVARIN—Quadruple fog flash (white), one minute intervals (new).

EAST CAPE—Fog flash—single white with single bomb, 30 sec. intervals (new).

MALAYAN ARCHIPELAGO lights unreliable owing eruptions. Lay from Somerset to Singapore direct, keeping highest levels.

For the Board:

CATTERTHUN
ST. JUST   } *Lights.*
VAN HEDDER

Casualties

Week ending Dec. 18th.

SABLE ISLAND LANDING TOWERS—Green freighter, number indistinguishable, up-ended, and fore-tank pierced after collision, passed 300-ft. level 2 p.m. Dec. 15th. Watched to water and pithed by Mark Boat.

N.F. BANKS—Postal Packet 162 reports *Halma* freighter (Fowey—St. John's) abandoned, leaking after weather, 46° 15' N. 50° 15' W. Crew rescued by Planet liner *Asteroid*. Watched to water and pithed by postal packet, Dec. 14th.

KERGEULEN MARK BOAT reports last call from *Cymena* freighter (Gayer Tong-Huk & Co.) taking water and sinking in snow-storm South McDonald Islands. No wreckage recovered. Addresses, etc., of crew at all A.B.C. offices.

FEZZAN—T.A.D. freighter *Ulema* taken ground during Harmattan on Akakus Range. Under plates strained. Crew at Ghat where repairing Dec. 13th.

BISCAY, MARK BOAT reports *Carducci* (Valandingham line) slightly spiked in western gorge Point de Benasque. Passengers transferred *Andorra* (same line). Barcelona Mark Boat salving cargo Dec. 12th.

ASCENSION, MARK BOAT—Wreck of unknown racing-plane, Parden rudder, wire-stiffened xylonite vans, and Harliss engine-seating, sighted and salved 7° 20' S. 18° 41' W. Dec. 15th. Photos at all A.B.C. offices.

Missing

No answer to General Call having been received during the last week from following overdues, they are posted as missing.

Atlantis, W. 17630 . . . . Canton–Valparaiso

Audhumla, W. 809. . . . . Stockholm–Odessa

Berenice, W. 2206 . . . . Riga–Vladivostock

Draco, E. 446   . . . . Coventry–Puntas Arenas

Tontine, E. 3068 . . . . C. Wrath–Ungava

Wu-Sung, E. 41776. . . . . Hankow–Lobito Bay

General Call (all Mark Boats) out for:

Jane Eyre, W. 6990 . . . . Port Rupert–City of Mexico

Santander, W. 5514 . . . . Gobi-desert–Manila

V. Edmundsun, E. 9690 . . . . Kandahar–Fiume

Broke for Obstruction, and Quitting Levels

VALKYRIE (racing plane), A. J. Hartley owner, New York (twice warned).

GEISHA (racing plane), S. van Cott owner, Philadelphia (twice warned).

MARVEL OF PERU (racing plane), J. X. Peixoto owner, Rio de Janeiro (twice warned).

For the Board:

LAZAREFF
McKEOUGH } *Traffic.*
GOLDBLATT

NOTES

High-Level Sleet

The Northern weather so far shows no sign of improvement. From all quarters come complaints of the unusual prevalence of sleet at the higher levels. Racing-planes and digs alike have suffered severely—the former from unequal deposits of half-frozen slush on their vans (and only those who have "held up" a badly balanced plane in a cross wind know what that means), and the latter from loaded bows and snow-cased bodies. As a consequence, the Northern and Northwestern upper levels have been practically abandoned, and the high fliers have returned to the ignoble security of the Three, Five, and Six hundred foot levels. But there remain a few undaunted sun-hunters who, in spite of frozen stays and ice-jammed connecting-rods, still haunt the blue empyrean.

Bat-Boat Racing

The scandals of the past few years have at last moved the yachting world to concerted action in regard to "bat" boat racing.

We have been treated to the spectacle of what are practically keeled racing-planes driven a clear five foot or more above the water, and only eased down to touch their so-called "native element" as they near the line. Judges and starters have been conveniently blind to this absurdity, but the public demonstration off St. Catherine's Light at the Autumn Regattas has borne ample, if tardy, fruit. In future the "bat" is to be a boat, and the long-unheeded demand of the true sportsman for "no daylight under mid-keel in smooth water" is in a fair way to be conceded. The new rule severely restricts plane area and lift alike. The gas compartments are permitted both fore and aft, as in the old type, but the water-ballast central tank is rendered obligatory. These things work, if not for perfection, at least for the evolution of a sane and wholesome *waterborne* cruiser. The type of rudder is unaffected by the new rules, so we may expect to see the Long-Davidson make (the patent on which has just expired) come largely into use henceforward, though the strain on the sternpost in turning at speeds over forty miles an hour is admittedly very severe. But bat-boat racing has a great future before it.

CORRESPONDENCE

Skylarking on the Equator

To the Editor—Only last week, while crossing the Equator (W. 26.15), I became aware of a furious and irregular cannonading some fifteen or twenty knots S. 4 E. Descending to the 500 ft. level, I found a party of Transylvanian tourists engaged in exploding scores of the largest pattern atmospheric bombs (A.B.C. standard) and, in the intervals of their pleasing labours, firing bow and stern smoke-ring swivels. This orgy—I can give it no other name—went on for at least two hours, and naturally produced violent electric derangements. My compasses, of course, were thrown out, my bow was struck twice, and I received two brisk shocks from the lower platform-rail. On remonstrating, I was told that these "professors" were engaged in scientific experiments. The extent of their "scientific" knowledge may be judged by the fact that they expected to produce (I give their own words) "a little blue sky" if "they went on long enough." This in the heart of the Doldrums at 450 feet! I have no objection to any amount of blue sky in its proper place (it can be found at the 2,000 level for practically twelve months out of the year), but I submit, with all deference to the educational needs of Transylvania, that "sky-larking" in the centre of a main-travelled road where, at the best of times, electricity literally drips off one's stanchions and screw blades, is unnecessary. When my friends had finished, the road was seared, and blown, and pitted with unequal pressure-layers, spirals, vortices, and readjustments for at least an hour. I pitched badly twice in an upward rush—solely due to these diabolical throw-downs—that came near to wrecking my propeller. Equatorial work at low levels is trying enough in all conscience without the added terrors of scientific hooliganism in the Doldrums.

Rhyl.
J. VINCENT MATHEWS.

[We entirely sympathize with Professor Mathews's views, but unluckily till the Board sees fit to further regulate the Southern areas in which scientific experiments may be conducted, we shall always be exposed to the risk which our correspondent describes. Unfortunately, a chimera bombinating in a vacuum is, nowadays, only too capable of producing secondary causes.—*Editor.*]

Answers to Correspondents

VIGILANS—The Laws of Auroral Derangements are still imperfectly understood. Any overheated motor may of course "seize" without warning; but so many complaints have reached us of accidents similar to yours while shooting the Aurora that we are inclined to believe with Lavalle that the upper strata of the Aurora Borealis are practically one big electric "leak," and that the paralysis of your engines was due to complete magnetization of all metallic parts. Low-flying planes often "glue up" when near the Magnetic Pole, and there is no reason in science why the same disability should not be experienced at higher levels when the Auroras are "delivering" strongly.

INDIGNANT—On your own showing, you were not under control. That you could not hoist the necessary N.U.C. lights on approaching a traffic-lane because your electrics had short-circuited is a misfortune which might befall any one. The A.B.C., being responsible for the planet's traffic, cannot, however, make allowance for this kind of misfortune. A reference to the Code will show that you were fined on the lower scale.

PLANISTON—(1) The Five Thousand Kilometre (overland) was won last year by L.V. Rautsch,

R.M. Rautsch, his brother, in the same week pulling off the Ten Thousand (oversea). R.M.'s average worked out at a fraction over 500 kilometres per hour, thus constituting a record. (2) Theoretically, there is no limit to the lift of a dirigible. For commercial and practical purposes 15,000 tons is accepted as the most manageable.

PATERFAMILIAS—None whatever. He is liable for direct damage both to your chimneys and any collateral damage caused by fall of bricks into garden, etc., etc. Bodily inconvenience and mental anguish may be included, but the average jury are not, as a rule, men of sentiment. If you can prove that his grapnel removed *any* portion of your roof, you had better rest your case on decoverture of domicile (See Parkins *v.* Duboulay). We entirely sympathize with your position, but the night of the 14th was stormy and confused, and—you may have to anchor on a stranger's chimney yourself some night. *Verbum sap!*

ALDEBARAN—War, as a paying concern, ceased in 1967. (2) The Convention of London expressly reserves to every nation the right of waging war so long as it does not interfere with the world's traffic. (3) The A.B.C. was constituted in 1949.

L.M.D.—Keep her dead head-on at half-power, taking advantage of the lulls to speed up and creep into it. She will strain much less this way than in quartering across a gale. (2) Nothing is to be gained by reversing into a following gale, and there is always risk of a turn-over. (3) The formulæ for stun'sle brakes are uniformly unreliable, and will continue to be so as long as air is compressible.

PEGAMOID—Personally we prefer glass or flux compounds to any other material for winter work nose-caps as being absolutely non-hygroscopic. (2) We cannot recommend any particular make.

PULMONAR—For the symptoms you describe, try the Gobi Desert Sanitaria. The low levels of the Saharan Sanitaria are against them except at the outset of the disease. (2) We do not recommend boarding-houses or hotels in this column.

BEGINNER—On still days the air above a large inhabited city being slightly warmer—i. e., thinner—than the atmosphere of the surrounding country, a plane drops a little on entering the rarefied area, precisely as a ship sinks a little in fresh water. Hence the phenomena of "jolt" and your "inexplicable collisions" with factory chimneys. In air, as on earth, it is safest to fly high.

EMERGENCY—There is only one rule of the road in air, earth, and water. Do you want the firmament to yourself?

PICCIOLA—Both Poles have been overdone in Art and Literature. Leave them to Science for the next twenty years. You did not send a stamp with your verses.

NORTH NIGERIA—The Mark Boat was within her right in warning you up on the Reserve. The shadow of a low-flying dirigible scares the game. You can buy all the photos you need at Sokoto.

NEW ERA—It is not etiquette to overcross an A.B.C. official's boat without asking permission. He is one of the body responsible for the planet's traffic, and for that reason must not be interfered with. You, presumably, are out on your own business or pleasure, and should leave him alone. For humanity's sake don't try to be "democratic."

REVIEWS

The Life of Xavier Lavalle

(*Reviewed by Réné Talland. École Aëronautique, Paris*)

Ten years ago Lavalle, "that imperturbable dreamer of the heavens," as Lazareff hailed him, gathered together the fruits of a lifetime's labour, and gave it, with well-justified contempt, to a world bound hand and foot to Barald's Theory of Vertices and "compensating electric nodes." "They shall see," he wrote—in that immortal postscript to "The Heart of the Cyclone"—"the Laws whose existence they derided written in fire *beneath* them."

"But even here," he continues, "there is no finality. Better a thousand times my conclusions should be discredited than that my dead name should lie across the threshold of the temple of Science—a bar to further inquiry."

So died Lavalle—a prince of the Powers of the Air, and even at his funeral Céllier jested at "him who had gone to discover the secrets of the Aurora Borealis."

If I choose thus to be banal, it is only to remind you that Céllier's theories are to-day as exploded as the ludicrous deductions of the Spanish school. In the place of their fugitive and warring dreams we have, definitely, Lavalle's Law of the Cyclone which he surprised in darkness and cold at the foot of the overarching throne of the Aurora Borealis. It is there that I, intent on my own investigations, have passed and re-passed a hundred times the worn leonine face, white as the snow beneath him, furrowed with wrinkles like the seams and gashes upon the North Cape; the nervous hand, integrally a part of the mechanism of his flighter; and above all, the wonderful lambent eyes turned to the zenith.

"Master," I would cry as I moved respectfully beneath him, "what is it you seek to-day?" and always the answer, clear and without doubt, from above: "The old secret, my son!"

The immense egotism of youth forced me on my own path, but (cry of the human always!) had I known—if I had known—I would many times have bartered my poor laurels for the privilege, such as Tinsley and Herrera possess, of having aided him in his monumental researches.

It is to the filial piety of Victor Lavalle that we owe the two volumes consecrated to the ground-life of his father, so full of the holy intimacies of the domestic hearth. Once returned from the abysms of the utter North to that little house upon the outskirts of Meudon, it was not the philosopher, the daring observer, the man of iron energy that imposed himself on his family, but a fat and even plaintive jester, a farceur incarnate and kindly, the co-equal of his children, and, it must be written, not seldom the comic despair of Madame Lavalle, who, as she writes five years after the marriage, to her venerable mother, found "in this unequalled intellect whose name I bear the abandon of a large and very untidy boy." Here is her letter:

"Xavier returned from I do not know where at midnight, absorbed in calculations on the eternal question of his Aurora—*la belle Aurore*, whom I begin to hate. Instead of anchoring—I had set out the guide-light above our roof, so he had but to descend and fasten the plane—he wandered, profoundly distracted, above the town with his anchor down! Figure to yourself, dear mother, it is the roof of the mayor's house that the grapnel first engages! That I do not regret, for the mayor's wife and I are not sympathetic; but when Xavier uproots my pet araucaria and bears it across the garden into the conservatory I protest at the top of my voice. Little Victor in his night-clothes runs to the window, enormously amused at the parabolic flight without reason, for it is too dark to see the grapnel, of my prized tree. The Mayor of Meudon thunders at our door in the name of the Law, demanding, I suppose, my husband's head. Here is the conversation through the megaphone—Xavier is two hundred feet above us.

"'Mons. Lavalle, descend and make reparation for outrage of domicile. Descend, Mons. Lavalle!'

"No one answers.

"'Xavier Lavalle, in the name of the Law, descend

and submit to process for outrage of domicile.'

"Xavier, roused from his calculations, only comprehending the last words: 'Outrage of domicile? My dear mayor, who is the man that has corrupted thy Julie?'

"The mayor, furious, 'Xavier Lavalle——'

"Xavier, interrupting: 'I have not that felicity. I am only a dealer in cyclones!'

"My faith, he raised one then! All Meudon attended in the streets, and my Xavier, after a long time comprehending what he had done, excused himself in a thousand apologies. At last the reconciliation was effected in our house over a supper at two in the morning—Julie in a wonderful costume of compromises, and I have her and the mayor pacified in beds in the blue room."

And on the next day, while the mayor rebuilds his roof, her Xavier departs anew for the Aurora Borealis, there to commence his life's work. M. Victor Lavalle tells us of that historic collision (*en plane*) on the flank of Hecla between Herrera, then a pillar of the Spanish school, and the man destined to confute his theories and lead him intellectually captive. Even through the years, the immense laugh of Lavalle as he sustains the Spaniard's wrecked plane, and cries: "Courage! *I* shall not fall till I have found Truth, and I hold *you* fast!" rings like the call of trumpets. This is that Lavalle whom the world, immersed in speculations of immediate gain, did not know nor suspect—the Lavalle whom they adjudged to the last a pedant and a theorist.

The human, as apart from the scientific, side (developed in his own volumes) of his epoch-making discoveries is marked with a simplicity, clarity, and good sense beyond praise. I would specially refer such as doubt the sustaining influence of ancestral faith upon character and will to the eleventh and nineteenth chapters, in which are contained the opening and consummation of the Tellurionical Records extending over nine years. Of their tremendous significance be sure that the modest house at Meudon knew as little as that the Records would one day be the world's standard in all official meteorology. It was enough for them that their Xavier—this son, this father, this husband—ascended periodically to commune with powers, it might be angelic, beyond their comprehension, and that they united daily in prayers for his safety.

"Pray for me," he says upon the eve of each of his excursions, and returning, with an equal simplicity, he renders thanks "after supper in the little room where he kept his barometers."

To the last Lavalle was a Catholic of the old school, accepting—he who had looked into the very heart of the lightnings—the dogmas of papal infallibility, of absolution, of confession—of relics great and small. Marvellous—enviable contradiction!

The completion of the Tellurionical Records closed what Lavalle himself was pleased to call the theoretical side of his labours—labours from which the youngest and least impressionable planeur might well have shrunk. He had traced through cold and heat, across the deeps of the oceans, with instruments of his own invention, over the inhospitable heart of the polar ice and the sterile visage of the deserts, league by league, patiently, unweariedly, remorselessly, from their ever-shifting cradle under the magnetic pole to their exalted death-bed in the utmost ether of the upper atmosphere—each one of the Isoconical Tellurions—Lavalle's Curves, as we call them to-day. He had disentangled the nodes of their intersections, assigning to each its regulated period of flux and reflux. Thus equipped, he summons Herrera and Tinsley, his pupils, to the final demonstration as calmly as though he were ordering his flighter for some midday journey to Marseilles.

"I have proved my thesis," he writes. "It remains now only that you should witness the proof. We go to Manila to-morrow. A cyclone will form off the Pescadores S. 17 E. in four days, and will reach its maximum intensity in twenty-seven hours after inception. It is there I will show you the Truth."

A letter heretofore unpublished from Herrera to Madame Lavalle tells us how the Master's prophecy was verified.

(*To be continued.*)

ADVERTISING SECTION

MISCELLANEOUS

WANTS

REQUIRED IMMEDIATELY, FOR East Africa, a thoroughly competent Plane and Dirigible Driver, acquainted with Petrol Radium and Helium motors and generators. Low-level work only, but must understand heavy-weight digs

MOSSAMEDES TRANSPORT ASSOC.

84 Palestine Buildings, E. C

MAN WANTED — DIG DRIVER for Southern Alps with Saharan summer trips. High levels, high speed, high wages.

Apply M. SIDNEY

Hotel San Stefano, Monte Carlo

FAMILY DIRIGIBLE. A COMPEtent, steady man wanted for slow speed, low level Tangye dirigible. No night work, no sea trips. Must be member of the Church of England, and make himself useful in the garden

M. R.,

The Rectory, Gray's Barton, Wilts.

COMMERCIAL DIG, CENTRAL and Southern Europe. A smart, active man for a L. M. T. Dig. Night work only. Headquarters London and Cairo. A linguist preferred.

BAGMAN

Charing Cross Hotel, W. C. (urgent.)

FOR SALE — A BARGAIN — SINgle Plane, narrow-gauge vans, Pinke motor. Restayed this autumn. Hansen air-kit, 38 in. chest, 15½ collar. Can be seen by appointment.

N. 2650. This office.

The Bee-Line Bookshop

BELT'S WAY-BOOKS, giving town lights for all towns over 4,000 pop. as laid down by A. B. C.

THE WORLD. Complete 2 vols. Thin Oxford, limp back. 12s. 6d.

BELT'S COASTAL ITINERARY. Shore Lights of the World. 7s. 6d.

THE TRANSATLANTIC AND MEDITERRANEAN TRAFFIC LINES. (By authority of the A.B.C.) Paper, 1s. 6d.; cloth, 2s. 6d. Ready Jan. 15.

ARCTIC AEROPLANING. Siemens and Galt. Cloth, bds. 3s. 6d.

LAVALLE'S HEART OF THE CYCLONE, with supplementary charts. 4s. 6d.

RIMINGTON'S PITFALLS IN THE AIR, and Table of Comparative Densities. 3s. 6d.

ANGELO'S DESERT IN A DIRIGIBLE. New edition, revised. 5s. 9d.

VAUGHAN'S PLANE RACING IN CALM AND STORM. 2s. 6d.

VAUGHAN'S HINTS TO THE AIRMATEUR. 1s.

HOFMAN'S LAWS OF LIFT AND VELOCITY. With diagrams, 3s. 6d.

DE VITRE'S THEORY OF SHIFTING BALLAST IN DIRIGIBLES. 2s. 6d.

SANGER'S WEATHERS OF THE WORLD. 4s.

SANGER'S TEMPERATURES AT HIGH ALTITUDES. 4s.

HAWKIN'S FOG AND HOW TO AVOID IT. 3s.

VAN ZUYLAN'S SECONDARY EFFECTS OF THUNDERSTORMS. 4s. 6d.

DAHLGREN'S AIR CURRENTS AND EPIDEMIC DISEASES. 5s. 6d.

REDMAYNE'S DISEASE AND THE BAROMETER. 7s. 6d.

WALTON'S HEALTH RESORTS OF THE GOBI AND SHAMO. 3s. 6d.

WALTON'S THE POLE AND PULMONARY COMPLAINTS. 7s. 6d.

MUTLOW'S HIGH LEVEL BACTERIOLOGY 7s. 6d.

HALLIWELL'S ILLUMINATED STAR MAP, with clockwork attachment, giving apparent motion of heavens, boxed, complete with clamps for binnacle, 36 inch size, only £2. 2. 0. (Invaluable for night work.) With A.B.C. certificate, £3. 10s. 0d.

Zalinski's Standard Works .

PASSES OF THE HIMALAYAS, 5s.
PASSES OF THE SIERRAS, 5s.
PASSES OF THE ROCKIES, 5s.
PASSES OF THE URALS, 5s.
The four boxed, limp cloth, with charts, 15s.

GRAY'S AIR CURRENTS IN MOUNTAIN GORGES. 7s. 6d.

A. C. BELT & SON, READING

BAT-BOATS

Flint & Mantel
Southampton

FOR SALE

at the end of Season the following Bat-Boats:

GRISELDA, 65 knt., 42 ft., 430 (nom.) Maginnis Motor, under-rake rudder.

MABELLE, 50 knt., 40 ft., 310 Hargreaves Motor, Douglas' lock-steering gear.

IVEMONA, 50 knt., 35 ft., 300 Hargreaves (Radium accelerator), Miller keel and rudder.

The above are well known on the South Coast as sound, wholesome knockabout boats, with ample cruising accommodation. *Griselda* carries spare set of Hofman racing vans and can be lifted three foot clear in smooth water with ballast-tank swung aft. The others do not lift clear of water, and are recommended for beginners.

Also, by private treaty, racing B. B. *Tarpon* (76 winning flags) 137 knt., 60 ft.; Long-Davidson double under-rake rudder, new this season and unstrained. 850 nom. Maginnis motor, Radium relays and Pond generator. Bronze breakwater forward, and treble reinforced forefoot and entry. Talfourd rockered keel. Triple set of Hofman vans, giving maximum lifting surface of 5327 sq. ft.

Tarpon has been lifted *and held* seven feet for two miles between touch and touch.

Our Autumn List of racing and family Bats ready on the 9th January.

ACCESSORIES AND SPARES

CHRISTIAN W

ESTA

Accessori

Hooded Binnacles with dip-dials automaticall
recording change of level (illuminated face).

All heights from 50 to 15,000 feet	£2	10
With Aerial Board of Control certificate	£3	11
Foot and Hand Foghorns; Sirens toned to any club note; with air-chest belt-driven from motor	£6	8
Wireless installations syntonised to A.B.C. requirements, in neat mahogany case, hundred mile range . . .	£3	3

Grapnels, mushroom anchors, pithing-iror
winches, hawsers, snaps, shackles and mooring rope
for lawn, city, and public installations.

Detachable under-cars, aluminum or stamped stee

Keeled under-cars for planes: single-action detac
ing-gear, turning car into boat with one motion
the wrist. Invaluable for sea trips.

Head, side, and riding lights (by size) Nos. 00
20 A.B.C. Standard. Rockets and fog-bombs
colours and tones of the principal clubs (boxed

A selection of twenty	£2	17
International night-signals (boxed)	£1	11

Catalogues fre

As Easy as A.B.C.

"[The A.B.C.], that semi-elected, semi-nominated body of a few score persons of both sexes, controls this planet. 'Transportation is Civilization,' our motto runs. Theoretically, we do what we please so long as we do not interfere with the traffic *and all it implies*. Practically, the A.B.C. confirms or annuls all international arrangements and, to judge from its last report, finds our tolerant, humorous, lazy little planet only too ready to shift the whole burden of private administration on its shoulders."—*With the Night Mail*

Isn't almost time that our planet took interest in the proceedings of the Aerial Board of Control? One knows that easy communications nowadays, and lack of privacy in the past, have killed all curiosity among mankind, but as the Board's Official Reporter I am bound to tell my tale.

At 9.30 A.M., August 26, A.D. 2065, the Board, sitting in London, was informed by De Forest that the District of Northern Illinois had riotously cut itself out of all systems and would remain disconnected till the Board should take over and administer it direct.

Every Northern Illinois freight and passenger tower was, he reported, out of action; all District main, local, and guiding lights had been extinguished; all General Communications were dumb, and through traffic had been diverted. No reason had been given, but he gathered unofficially from the Mayor of Chicago that the District complained of 'crowd-making and invasion of privacy.'

As a matter of fact, it is of no importance whether Northern Illinois stay in or out of planetary circuit; as a matter of policy, any complaint of invasion of privacy needs immediate investigation, lest worse follow.

By 9.45 A.M. De Forest, Dragomiroff (Russia), Takahira (Japan), and Pirolo (Italy) were empowered to visit Illinois and 'to take such steps as might be necessary for the resumption of traffic *and all that that implies.*' By 10 A.M. the Hall was empty, and the four Members and I were aboard what Pirolo insisted on calling 'my leetle godchild'—that is to say, the new *Victor Pirolo.* Our Planet prefers to know Victor Pirolo as a gentle, grey-haired enthusiast who spends his time near Foggia, inventing or creating new breeds of Spanish-Italian olive-trees; but there is another side to his nature—the manufacture of quaint inventions, of which the *Victor Pirolo* is perhaps, not

92

the least surprising. She and a few score sister-craft of the same type embody his latest ideas. But she is not comfortable. An A.B.C. boat does not take the air with the level-keeled lift of a liner, but shoots up rocket-fashion like the 'aeroplane' of our ancestors, and makes her height at top-speed from the first. That is why I found myself sitting suddenly on the large lap of Eustace Arnott, who commands the A.B.C. Fleet. One knows vaguely that there is such a thing as a Fleet somewhere on the Planet, and that, theoretically, it exists for the purposes of what used to be known as 'war.' Only a week before, while visiting a glacier sanatorium behind Gothaven, I had seen some squadrons making false auroras far to the north while they manoeuvred round the Pole; but, naturally, it had never occurred to me that the things could be used in earnest.

Said Arnott to De Forest as I staggered to a seat on the chart-room divan: 'We're tremendously grateful to 'em in Illinois. We've never had a chance of exercising all the Fleet together. I've turned in a General Call, and I expect we'll have at least two hundred keels aloft this evening.'

'Well aloft?' De Forest asked.

'Of course, sir. Out of sight till they're called for.'

Arnott laughed as he lolled over the transparent chart-table where the map of the summer-blue

Atlantic slid along, degree by degree, in exact answer to our progress. Our dial already showed 320 m.p.h. and we were two thousand feet above the uppermost traffic lines.

'Now, where is this Illinois District of yours?' said Dragomiroff. 'One travels so much, one sees so little. Oh, I remember! It is in North America.'

De Forest, whose business it is to know the out districts, told us that it lay at the foot of Lake Michigan, on a road to nowhere in particular, was about half an hour's run from end to end, and, except in one corner, as flat as the sea. Like most flat countries nowadays, it was heavily guarded against invasion of privacy by forced timber—fifty-foot spruce and tamarack, grown in five years. The population was close on two millions, largely migratory between Florida and California, with a backbone of small farms (they call a thousand acres a farm in Illinois) whose owners come into Chicago for amusements and society during the winter. They were, he said noticeably kind, quiet folk, but a little exacting, as all flat countries must be, in their notions of privacy. There had, for instance, been no printed news-sheet in Illinois for twenty-seven years. Chicago argued that engines for printed news sooner or later developed into engines for invasion of privacy, which in turn might bring the old terror of Crowds and blackmail back to the Planet. So news-sheets were not.

'And that's Illinois,' De Forest concluded. 'You see, in the Old Days, she was in the fore-front of what they used to call "progress," and Chicago—'

'Chicago?' said Takahira. 'That's the little place where there is Salati's Statue of the Nigger in Flames. A fine bit of old work.'

'When did you see it?' asked De Forest quickly. 'They only unveil it once a year.'

'I know. At Thanksgiving. It was then,' said Takahira, with a shudder. 'And they sang "Mac-Donough's Song," too.'

'Whew!' De Forest whistled. 'I did not know that! I wish you'd told me before. "MacDonough's Song" may have had its uses when it was com-posed, but it was an infernal legacy for any man to leave behind.'

'It's protective instinct, my dear fellows,' said Pi-rolo, rolling a cigarette. 'The Planet, she has had her dose of popular government. She suffers from inherited agoraphobia. She has no—ah—use for crowds.'

Dragomiroff leaned forward to give him a light. 'Certainly,' said the white-bearded Russian, 'the Planet has taken all precautions against crowds for the past hundred years. What is our total pop-ulation today? Six hundred million, we hope; five hundred, we think; but—but if next year's census shows more than four hundred and fifty, I myself will eat all the extra little babies. We have cut the birth-rate out—right out! For a long time we have said to Almighty God, "Thank You, Sir, but we do not much like Your game of life, so we will not play." '

'Anyhow,' said Arnott defiantly, 'men live a century apiece on the average now.'

'Oh, that is quite well! I am rich—you are rich—we are all rich and happy because we are so few and we live so long. Only I think Almighty God He will remember what the Planet was like in the time of Crowds and the Plague. Perhaps He will send us nerves. Eh, Pirolo?'

The Italian blinked into space. 'Perhaps,' he said, 'He has sent them already. Anyhow, you cannot argue with the Planet. She does not forget the Old Days, and—what can you do?'

'For sure we can't remake the world.' De Forest glanced at the map flowing smoothly across the table from west to east. 'We ought to be over our ground by nine to-night. There won't be much sleep afterwards.'

On which hint we dispersed, and I slept till Takahira waked me for dinner. Our ancestors thought nine hours' sleep ample for their little lives. We, living thirty years longer, feel ourselves defrauded with less than eleven out of the twenty-four.

By ten o'clock we were over Lake Michigan. The west shore was lightless, except for a dull ground-glare at Chicago, and a single traffic-directing light—its leading beam pointing north—at Waukegan on our starboard bow. None of the Lake villages gave any sign of life; and inland, westward, so far as we could see, blackness lay unbroken on the level earth. We swooped down and skimmed low across the dark, throwing calls county by county. Now and again we picked up the faint glimmer of a house-light, or heard the rasp and rend of a cultivator being played across the fields, but Northern Illinois as a whole was one inky, apparently uninhabited, waste of high, forced woods. Only our illuminated map, with its little pointer switching from county to county, as we wheeled and twisted, gave us any idea of our position. Our calls, urgent, pleading, coaxing or commanding, through the General Communicator brought no answer. Illinois strictly maintained her own privacy in the timber which she grew for that purpose.

'Oh, this is absurd!' said De Forest. 'We're like an owl trying to work a wheat-field. Is this Bureau Creek? Let's land, Arnott, and get hold of some one.'

We brushed over a belt of forced woodland— fifteen-year-old maple sixty feet high—grounded on a private meadow-dock, none too big, where we moored to our own grapnels, and hurried out through the warm dark night towards a light in a verandah. As we neared the garden gate I could have sworn we had stepped knee-deep in quick-sand, for we could scarcely drag our feet against the prickling currents that clogged them. After five paces we stopped, wiping our foreheads, as hopelessly stuck on dry smooth turf as so many cows in a bog.

'Pest!' cried Pirolo angrily. We are ground-circuited. And it is my own system of ground-circuits too! I know the pull.'

'Good evening,' said a girl's voice from the verandah. 'Oh, I'm sorry! We've locked up. Wait a minute.'

We heard the click of a switch, and almost fell forward as the currents round our knees were withdrawn.

The girl laughed, and laid aside her knitting. An old-fashioned Controller stood at her elbow, which she reversed from time to time, and we could hear the snort and clank of the obedient cultivator half a mile away, behind the guardian woods.

'Come in and sit down,' she said. 'I'm only playing a plough. Dad's gone to Chicago to—Ah! Then it was *your* call I heard just now!'

She had caught sight of Arnott's Board uniform, leaped to the switch, and turned it full on.

We were checked, gasping, waist-deep in current this time, three yards from the verandah.

'We only want to know what's the matter with Illinois,' said De Forest placidly.

'Then hadn't you better go to Chicago and find out?' she answered. 'There's nothing wrong here. We own ourselves.'

'How can we go anywhere if you won't loose us?' De Forest went on, while Arnott scowled. Admirals of Fleets are still quite human when their dignity is touched.

'Stop a minute—you don't know how funny you look!' She put her hands on her hips and laughed mercilessly.

'Don't worry about that,' said Arnott, and whistled. A voice answered from the *Victor Pirolo* in the meadow.

'Only a single-fuse ground-circuit!' Arnott called. 'Sort it out gently, please.'

We heard the ping of a breaking lamp; a fuse blew out somewhere in the verandah roof, frightening a nest full of birds. The groud-circuit was open. We stooped and rubbed our tingling ankles.

'How rude—how very rude of you!' the maiden cried.

'Sorry, but we haven't time to look funny,' said Arnott. 'We've got to go to Chicago; and if I were you, young lady, I'd go into the cellars for the next two hours, and take mother with me.'

Off he strode, with us at his heels, muttering indignantly, till the humour of the thing struck and doubled him up with laughter at the foot of the gangway ladder.

'The Board hasn't shown what you might call a fat spark on this occasion,' said De Forest, wiping his eyes. 'I hope I didn't look as big a fool as you did, Arnott! Hullo! What on earth is that? Dad coming home from Chicago?'

There was a rattle and a rush, and a five-plough cultivator, blades in air like so many teeth, trundled itself at us round the edge of the timber, fuming and sparking furiously.

'Jump!' said Arnott, as we hurled ourselves through the none-too-wide door. 'Never mind about shutting it. Up!'

The *Victor Pirolo* lifted like a bubble, and the vicious machine shot just underneath us, clawing high as it passed.

'There's a nice little spit-kitten for you!' said Arnott, dusting his knees. 'We ask her a civil question. First she circuits us and then she plays a cultivator at us!'

'And then we fly,' said Dragomiroff. 'If I were forty years more young, I would go back and kiss her. Ho! Ho!'

'I,' said Pirolo, 'would smack her! My pet ship has been chased by a dirty plough; a—how do you say?—agricultural implement.'

'Oh, that is Illinois all over,' said De Forest. 'They don't content themselves with talking about privacy. They arrange to have it. And now, where's your alleged fleet, Arnott? We must assert ourselves against this wench.'

Arnott pointed to the black heavens. 'Waiting on—up there,' said he. 'Shall I give them the whole installation, sir?'

'Oh, I don't think the young lady is quite worth that,' said De Forest. 'Get over Chicago, and perhaps we'll see something.'

In a few minutes we were hanging at two thousand feet over an oblong block of incandescence in the centre of the little town.

'That looks like the old City Hall. Yes, there's Salati's Statue in front of it,' said Takahira.

'But what on earth are they doing to the place? I thought they used it for a market nowadays! Drop a little, please.'

We could hear the sputter and crackle of road-surfacing machines—the cheap Western type which fuse stone and rubbish into lava-like ribbed glass for their rough country roads. Three or four surfacers worked on each side of a square of ruins. The brick and stone wreckage crumbled, slid forward, and presently spread out into white-hot pools of sticky slag, which the levelling-rods smoothed more or less flat. Already a third of the big block had been so treated, and was cooling to dull red before our astonished eyes.

'It is the Old Market,' said De Forest. 'Well, there's nothing to prevent Illinois from making a road through a market. It doesn't interfere with traffic, that I can see.'

'Hsh!' said Arnott, gripping me by the shoulder. 'Listen! They're singing. Why on the earth are they singing?'

We dropped again till we could see the black fringe of people at the edge of that glowing square.

At first they only roared against the roar of the surfacers and levellers. Then the words came up clearly—the words of the Forbidden Song that all men knew, and none let pass their lips—poor Pat MacDonough's Song, made in the days of the Crowds and the Plague—every silly word of it loaded to sparking-point with the Planet's inherited memories of horror, panic, fear and cruelty. And Chicago—innocent, contented little Chicago—was singing it aloud to the infernal tune that carried riot, pestilence and lunacy round our Planet a few generations ago!

'Once there was The People—Terror gave it birth;
Once there was The People, and it made a hell of earth!'

(Then the stamp and pause):

'Earth arose and crushed it. Listen, oh, ye slain!

Once there was The People—it shall never be again!'

The levellers thrust in savagely against the ruins as the song renewed itself again, again and again, louder than the crash of the melting walls.

De Forest frowned. 'I don't like that,' he said. 'They've broken back to the Old Days! They'll be killing somebody soon. I think we'd better divert 'em, Arnott.'

'Ay, ay, sir.' Arnott's hand went to his cap, and we heard the hull of the *Victor Pirolo* ring to the command: 'Lamps! Both watches stand by! Lamps! Lamps! Lamps!'

'Keep still!' Takahira whispered to me. 'Blinkers, please, quartermaster.'

'It's all right—all right!' said Pirolo from behind, and to my horror slipped over my head some sort of rubber helmet that locked with a snap. I could feel thick colloid bosses before my eyes, but I stood in absolute darkness.

'To save the sight,' he explained, and pushed me on to the chart-room divan. 'You will see in a minute.'

As he spoke I became aware of a thin thread of almost intolerable light, let down from heaven at an immense distance—one vertical hair's breadth of frozen lightning.

'Those are our flanking ships,' said Arnott at my elbow. 'That one is over Galena. Look south—that other one's over Keithburg. Vincennes is behind us, and north yonder is Winthrop Woods. The Fleet's in position, sir'—this to De Forest. 'As soon as you give the word.'

'Ah no! No!' cried Dragomiroff at my side. I could feel the old man tremble. 'I do not know all that you can do, but be kind! I ask you to be a little kind to them below! This is horrible horrible!'

'"When a Woman kills a Chicken,/Dynasties and Empires sicken,"' Takahira quoted. 'It is too late to be gentle now.'

'Then take off my helmet! Take off my helmet!' Dragomiroff began hysterically.

Pirolo must have put his arm round him.

'Hush,' he said, 'I am here. It is all right, Ivan, my dear fellow.'

'I'll just send our little girl in Bureau County a warning,' said Arnott. 'She don't deserve it, but we'll allow her a minute or two to take mamma to the cellar.'

In the utter hush that followed the growling spark after Arnott had linked up his Service Communicator with the invisible Fleet, we heard "MacDonough's Song" from the city beneath us grow fainter as we rose to position. Then I clapped my hand before my mask lenses, for it was as though the floor of Heaven had been riddled and all the inconceivable blaze of suns in the making was poured through the manholes.

'You needn't count,' said Arnott. I had had no thought of such a thing. 'There are two hundred and fifty keels up there, five miles apart. Full power, please, for another twelve seconds.'

The firmament, as far as eye could reach, stood on pillars of white fire. One fell on the glowing square at Chicago, and turned it black.

'Oh! Oh! Oh! Can men be allowed to do such things?' Dragomiroff cried, and fell across our knees.

'Glass of water, please,' said Takahira to a helmeted shape that leaped forward. 'He is a little faint.'

The lights switched off, and the darkness stunned like an avalanche. We could hear Dragomiroff's teeth on the glass edge.

Pirolo was comforting him.

'All right, all ra-ight,' he repeated. 'Come and lie down. Come below and take off your mask. I give you my word, old friend, it is all right. They are my siege-lights. Little *Victor Pirolo*'s leetle lights. You know me! I do not hurt people.'

'Pardon!' Dragomiroff moaned. 'I have never seen Death. I have never seen the Board take action. Shall we go down and burn them alive, or is that already done?'

'Oh, hush,' said Pirolo, and I think he rocked him in his arms.

'Do we repeat, sir?' Arnott asked De Forest.

'Give 'em a minute's break,' De Forest replied.' They may need it.'

We waited a minute, and then "MacDonough's Song," broken but defiant, rose from undefeated Chicago.

'They seem fond of that tune,' said De Forest. 'I should let 'em have it, Arnott.'

'Very good, sir,' said Arnott, and felt his way to the Communicator keys.

No lights broke forth, but the hollow of the skies made herself the mouth for one note that touched the raw fibre of the brain. Men hear such sounds in delirium, advancing like tides from horizons beyond the ruled foreshores of space.

'That's our pitch-pipe,' said Arnott. 'We may be a bit ragged. I've never conducted two hundred and fifty performers before.' He pulled out the couplers, and struck a full chord on the Service Communicators.

The beams of light leaped down again, and danced, solemnly and awfully, a stilt-dance, sweeping thirty or forty miles left and right at each stiff-legged kick, while the darkness delivered itself—there is no scale to measure against that utterance—of the tune to which they kept time. Certain notes—one learnt to expect them with terror—cut through one's marrow, but, after three minutes, thought and emotion passed in indescribable agony.

We saw, we heard, but I think we were in some sort swooning. The two hundred and fifty beams shifted, re-formed, straddled and split, narrowed, widened, rippled in ribbons, broke into a thousand white-hot parallel lines, melted and revolved in interwoven rings like old-fashioned engine-turning, flung up to the zenith, made as if to descend and renew the torment, halted at the last instant, twizzled insanely round the horizon, and vanished, to bring back for the hundredth time darkness more shattering than their instantly renewed light over all Illinois. Then the tune and lights ceased together, and we heard one single devastating wail that shook all the horizon as a rubbed wet finger shakes the rim of a bowl.

'Ah, that is my new siren,' said Pirolo. 'You can break an iceberg in half, if you find the proper pitch. They will whistle by squadrons now. It is the wind through pierced shutters in the bows.'

I had collapsed beside Dragomiroff, broken and snivelling feebly, because I had been delivered before my time to all the terrors of Judgment Day, and the Archangels of the Resurrection were hail-ing me naked across the Universe to the sound of the music of the spheres.

Then I saw De Forest smacking Arnott's helmet with his open hand. The wailing died down in a long shriek as a black shadow swooped past us, and returned to her place above the lower clouds.

'I hate to interrupt a specialist when he's enjoying himself,' said De Forest. 'But, as a matter of fact, all Illinois has been asking us to stop for these last fifteen seconds.'

'What a pity.' Arnott slipped off his mask. 'I wanted you to hear us really hum. Our lower C can lift street-paving.'

'It is Hell—Hell!' cried Dragomiroff, and sobbed aloud.

Arnott looked away as he answered: 'It's a few thousand volts ahead of the old shoot-'em-and-sink-'em game, but I should scarcely call it that. What shall I tell the Fleet, sir?'

'Tell 'em we're very pleased and impressed. I don't think they need wait on any longer. There isn't a spark left down there.' De Forest pointed. 'They'll be deaf and blind.'

'Oh, I think not, sir. The demonstration lasted less than ten minutes.'

'Marvellous!' Takahira sighed. 'I should have said it was half a night. Now, shall we go down and pick up the pieces?'

'But first a small drink,' said Pirolo. 'The Board must not arrive weeping at its own works.'

'I am an old fool—an old fool!' Dragomiroff began piteously. 'I did not know what would happen. It is all new to me. We reason with them in Little Russia.'

Chicago North landing-tower was unlighted, and Arnott worked his ship into the clips by her own lights. As soon as these broke out we heard groanings of horror and appeal from many people below.

'All right,' shouted Arnott into the darkness. 'We aren't beginning again!' We descended by the stairs, to find ourselves knee deep in a grovelling crowd, some crying that they were blind, others beseeching us not to make any more noises, but the greater part writhing face downward, their hands or their caps before their eyes.

It was Pirolo who came to our rescue. He climbed the side of a surfacing-machine, and there, gesticulating as though they could see, made oration to those afflicted people of Illinois.

'You stchewpids!' he began. 'There is nothing to fuss for. Of course, your eyes will smart and be red to-morrow. You will look as if you and your wives had drunk too much, but in a little while you will see again as well as before. I tell you this, and I—I am Pirolo. Victor Pirolo!'

The crowd with one accord shuddered, for many legends attach to Victor Pirolo of Foggia, deep in the secrets of God.

'Pirolo?' An unsteady voice lifted itself. 'Then tell us was there anything except light in those lights of yours just now?'

The question was repeated from every corner of the darkness.

Pirolo laughed.

'No!' he thundered. (Why have small men such large voices?) 'I give you my word and the Board's word that there was nothing except light—just light! You stchewpids! Your birth-rate is too low already as it is. Some day I must invent something to send it up, but send it down—never!'

'Is that true?—We thought—somebody said—'

One could feel the tension relax all round.

'You too big fools,' Pirolo cried. 'You could have sent us a call and we would have told you.'

'Send you a call!' a deep voice shouted. 'I wish you had been at our end of the wire.'

'I'm glad I wasn't,' said De Forest. 'It was bad enough from behind the lamps. Never mind! It's over now. Is there any one here I can talk business with? I'm De Forest—for the Board.'

'You might begin with me, for one—I'm Mayor,' the bass voice replied.

A big man rose unsteadily from the street, and

staggered towards us where we sat on the broad turf-edging, in front of the garden fences.

'I ought to be the first on my feet. Am I?' said he.

'Yes,' said De Forest, and steadied him as he dropped down beside us.

'Hello, Andy. Is that you?' a voice called.

'Excuse me,' said the Mayor; 'that sounds like my Chief of Police, Bluthner!'

'Bluthner it is; and here's Mulligan and Keefe— on their feet.'

'Bring 'em up please, Blut. We're supposed to be the Four in charge of this hamlet. What we says, goes. And, De Forest, what do you say?'

'Nothing—yet,' De Forest answered, as we made room for the panting, reeling men. 'You've cut out of system. Well?'

'Tell the steward to send down drinks, please,' Arnott whispered to an orderly at his side.

'Good!' said the Mayor, smacking his dry lips. 'Now I suppose we can take it, De Forest, that henceforward the Board will administer us direct?'

'Not if the Board can avoid it,' De Forest laughed. 'The A.B.C. is responsible for the planetary traffic only.'

'*And all that that implies.*' The Big Four who ran Chicago chanted their *Magna Charta* like children at school.

'Well, get on,' said De Forest wearily. 'What is your silly trouble anyway?'

'Too much dam' Democracy,' said the Mayor, laying his hand on De Forest's knee.

'So? I thought Illinois had had her dose of that.'

'She has. That's why. Blut, what did you do with our prisoners last night?'

'Locked 'em in the water-tower to prevent the women killing 'em,' the Chief of Police replied. 'I'm too blind to move just yet, but—'

'Arnott, send some of your people, please, and fetch 'em along,' said De Forest.

'They're triple-circuited,' the Mayor called. 'You'll have to blow out three fuses.' He turned to De Forest, his large outline just visible in the paling darkness. 'I hate to throw any more work on the Board. I'm an administrator myself, but we've had a little fuss with our Serviles. What? In a big city there's bound to be a few men and women who can't live without listening to themselves, and who prefer drinking out of pipes they don't own both ends of. They inhabit flats and hotels all the year round. They say it saves 'em trouble. Anyway, it gives 'em more time to make trouble for their neighbours. We call 'em Serviles locally. And they are apt to be tuberculous.'

'Just so!' said the man called Mulligan. 'Transportation is Civilisation. Democracy is Disease. I've proved it by the blood-test, every time.'

'Mulligan's our Health Officer, and a one-idea man,' said the Mayor, laughing. 'But it's true that most Serviles haven't much control. They will talk; and when people take to talking as a business, anything may arrive—mayn't it, De Forest?'

'Anything—except the facts of the case,' said De Forest, laughing.

'I'll give you those in a minute,' said the Mayor. 'Our Serviles got to talking—first in their houses and then on the streets, telling men and women how to manage their own affairs. (You can't teach a Servile not to finger his neighbour's soul.) That's invasion of privacy, of course, but in Chicago we'll suffer anything sooner than make crowds. Nobody took much notice, and so I let 'em alone. My fault! I was warned there would be trouble, but there hasn't been a crowd or murder in Illinois for nineteen years.'

'Twenty-two,' said his Chief of Police.

'Likely. Anyway, we'd forgot such things. So, from talking in the houses and on the streets, our Serviles go to calling a meeting at the Old Market yonder.' He nodded across the square where the wrecked buildings heaved up grey in the dawn-glimmer behind the square-cased statue of The Negro in Flames. 'There's nothing to prevent any-

one calling meetings except that it's against human nature to stand in a crowd, besides being bad
for the health. I ought to have known by the way
our men and women attended that first meeting
that trouble was brewing. There were as many as
a thousand in the market-place, touching each
other. Touching! Then the Serviles turned in all
tongue-switches and talked, and we—'

'What did they talk about?' said Takahira.

'First, how badly things were managed in the
city. That pleased us Four—we were on the platform—because we hoped to catch one or two
good men for City work. You know how rare
executive capacity is. Even if we didn't it's—it's
refreshing to find any one interested enough in
our job to damn our eyes. You don't know what it
means to work, year in, year out, without a spark
of difference with a living soul.'

'Oh, don't we!' said De Forest. 'There are times
on the Board when we'd give our positions if any
one would kick us out and take hold of things
themselves.'

'But they won't,' said the Mayor ruefully. 'I as-
sure you, sir, we Four have done things in Chicago, in the hope of rousing people, that would have
discredited Nero. But what do they say? "Very
good, Andy. Have it your own way. Anything's
better than a crowd. I'll go back to my land." You

114

can't do anything with folk who can go where they please, and don't want anything on God's earth except their own way. There isn't a kick or a kicker left on the Planet.'

'Then I suppose that little shed yonder fell down by itself?' said De Forest. We could see the bare and still smoking ruins, and hear the slag-pools crackle as they hardened and set.

'Oh, that's only amusement. Tell you later. As I was saying, our Serviles held the meeting, and pretty soon we had to ground-circuit the platform to save 'em from being killed. And that didn't make our people any more pacific.'

'How d'you mean?' I ventured to ask.

'If you've ever been ground-circuited,' said the Mayor, 'you'll know it don't improve any man's temper to be held up straining against nothing. No, sir! Eight or nine hundred folk kept pawing and buzzing like flies in treacle for two hours, while a pack of perfectly safe Serviles invades their mental and spiritual privacy, may be amusing to watch, but they are not pleasant to handle afterwards.'

Pirolo chuckled.

'Our folk own themselves. They were of opinion things were going too far and too fiery. I warned the Serviles; but they're born house-dwellers. Unless a fact hits 'em on the head, they cannot see it. Would you believe me, they went on to talk of what they called "popular government"? They did! They wanted us to go back to the old Voo-doo-business of voting with papers and wooden boxes, and word-drunk people and printed for-mulas, and news-sheets! They said they practised it among themselves about what they'd have to eat in their flats and hotels. Yes, sir! They stood up behind Bluthner's doubled ground-circuits, and they said that, in this present year of grace, to self-owning men and women, on that very spot! Then they finished'—he lowered his voice cautiously—'by talking about "The People." And then Bluthner he had to sit up all night in charge of the circuits because he couldn't trust his men to keep 'em shut.'

'It was trying 'em too high,' the Chief of Police broke in. 'But we couldn't hold the crowd ground-circuited for ever. I gathered in all the Serviles on charge of crowd-making, and put 'em in the wa-ter-tower, and then I let things cut loose. I had to! The District lit like a sparked gas-tank!'

'The news was out over seven degrees of coun-try,' the Mayor continued; 'and when once it's a question of invasion of privacy, good-bye to right and reason in Illinois! They began turning out traffic-lights and locking up landing-towers on Thursday night. Friday, they stopped all traffic and asked for the Board to take over. Then they wanted to clean Chicago off the side of the Lake and rebuild elsewhere—just for a souvenir of "The People" that the Serviles talked about. I suggested that they should slag the Old Market where the meeting was held, while I turned in a call to you all on the Board. That kept 'em quiet till you came along. And—and now you can take hold of the situation.'

'Any chance of their quieting down?' De Forest asked.

'You can try,' said the Mayor.

De Forest raised his voice in the face of the reviving crowd that had edged in towards us. Day was come.

'Don't you think this business can be arranged?' he began. But there was a roar of angry voices:

'We've finished with Crowds! We aren't going back to the Old Days! Take us over! Take the Serviles away! Administer direct or we'll kill 'em! Down with The People!'

An attempt was made to begin "MacDonough's Song." It got no further than the first line, for the *Victor Pirolo* sent down a warning drone on one stopped horn. A wrecked side-wall of the Old Market tottered and fell inwards on the slag-pools. None spoke or moved till the last of the dust had settled down again, turning the steel case of Salati's Statue ashy grey.

'You see you'll just have to take us over', the Mayor whispered.

De Forest shrugged his shoulders.

'You talk as if executive capacity could be snatched out of the air like so much horse-power. Can't you manage yourselves on any terms?' he said.

'We can, if you say so. It will only cost those few lives to begin with.'

The Mayor pointed across the square, where Arnott's men guided a stumbling group of ten or twelve men and women to the lake front and halted them under the Statue.

'Now I think,' said Takahira under his breath, 'there will be trouble.'

The mass in front of us growled like beasts.

At that moment the sun rose clear, and revealed the blinking assembly to itself. As soon as it realised that it was a crowd we saw the shiver of horror and mutual repulsion shoot across it precisely as the steely flaws shot across the lake outside. Nothing was said, and, being half blind, of course it moved slowly. Yet in less than fifteen minutes most of that vast multitude—three thousand at the lowest count—melted away like frost on south eaves. The remnant stretched themselves on the grass, where a crowd feels and looks less like a crowd.

'These mean business,' the Mayor whispered to Takahira. 'There are a goodish few women there who've borne children. I don't like it.'

The morning draught off the lake stirred the trees round us with promise of a hot day; the sun reflected itself dazzlingly on the canister-shaped covering of Salati's Statue; cocks crew in the gardens, and we could hear gate-latches clicking in the distance as people stumblingly resought their homes.

'I'm afraid there won't be any morning deliveries,' said De Forest. 'We rather upset things in the country last night.'

'That makes no odds,' the Mayor returned. 'We're all provisioned for six months. We take no chances.'

Nor, when you come to think of it, does anyone else. It must be three-quarters of a generation since any house or city faced a food shortage. Yet is there house or city on the Planet today that has not half a year's provisions laid in? We are like the shipwrecked seamen in the old books, who, having once nearly starved to death, ever afterwards hide away bits of food and biscuit. Truly we trust no Crowds, nor system based on Crowds!

De Forest waited till the last footstep had died away. Meantime the prisoners at the base of the Statue shuffled, posed and fidgeted, with the shamelessness of quite little children. None of them were more than six feet high, and many of them were as grey-haired as the ravaged, harassed heads of old pictures. They huddled together in actual touch, while the crowd, spaced at large intervals, looked at them with congested eyes.

Suddenly a man among them began to talk. The Mayor had not in the least exaggerated. It appeared that our Planet lay sunk in slavery beneath the heel of the Aerial Board of Control. The orator urged us to arise in our might, burst our prison doors and break our fetters (all his metaphors, by the way, were of the most medieval). Next he demanded that every matter of daily life, including most of the physical functions, should be submitted for decision at any time of the week, month, or year to, I gathered, anybody who happened to be passing by or residing within a certain radius, and that everybody should forthwith abandon his concerns to settle the matter, first by crowd-making, next by talking to the crowds made, and lastly by describing crosses on pieces of paper, which rubbish should later be counted with certain mystic ceremonies and oaths. Out of this amazing play, he assured us, would automatically arise a higher, nobler, and kinder world, based— he demonstrated this with the awful lucidity of the insane—based on the sanctity of the Crowd and the villainy of the single person. In conclusion, he called loudly upon God to testify to his personal merits and integrity. When the flow ceased, I turned bewildered to Takahira, who was nodding solemnly.

'Quite correct,' said he 'It is all in the old books. He has left nothing out, not even the war-talk.'

'But I don't see how this stuff can upset a child, much less a district,' I replied.

'Ah, you are too young,' said Dragomiroff. 'For another thing, you are not a mamma. Please look at the mammas.'

Ten or fifteen women who remained had separated themselves from the silent men, and were drawing in towards the prisoners. It reminded one of the stealthy encircling, before the rush in at the quarry, of wolves round musk oxen in the North. The prisoners saw, and drew together more closely. The Mayor covered his face with his hands for an instant. De Forest, bareheaded, stepped forward between the prisoners and the slowly, stiffly moving line.

'That's all very interesting,' he said to the dry-lipped orator. 'But the point seems that you've been making crowds and invading privacy.'

A woman stepped forward, and would have spoken, but there was a quick assenting murmur from the men, who realised that De Forest was trying to pull the situation down to ground-line.

'Yes! Yes!' they cried. 'We cut out because they made crowds and invaded privacy! Stick to that! Keep on that switch! Lift the Serviles out of this! The Board's in charge! Hsh!'

'Yes, the Board's in charge,' said De Forest.

'I'll take formal evidence of crowd-making if you like, but the Members of the Board can testify to it. Will that do?'

The women had closed in another pace, with hands that clenched and unclenched at their sides.

'Good! Good enough!' the men cried. 'We're content. Only take them away quickly.'

'Come along up!' said De Forest to the captives. 'Breakfast is quite ready.'

It appeared, however, that they did not wish to go. They intended to remain in Chicago and make crowds. They pointed out that De Forest's proposal was gross invasion of privacy.

'My dear fellow,' said Pirolo to the most voluble of the leaders, 'you hurry, or your crowd that can't be wrong will kill you!'

'But that would be murder,' answered the believer in crowds; and there was a roar of laughter from all sides that seemed to show the crisis had broken.

A woman stepped forward from the line of women, laughing, I protest, as merrily as any of the company. One hand, of course, shaded her eyes, the other was at her throat.

'Oh, they needn't be afraid of being killed!' she called.

'Not in the least,' said De Forest. 'But don't you think that, now the Board's in charge, you might go home while we get these people away?'

'I shall be home long before that. It—it has been rather a trying day.'

She stood up to her full height, dwarfing even De Forest's six-foot-eight, and smiled, with eyes closed against the fierce light.

'Yes, rather,' said De Forest. 'I'm afraid you feel the glare a little. We'll have the ship down.'

He motioned to the Pirolo to drop between us and the sun, and at the same time to loop-circuit the prisoners, who were a trifle unsteady. We saw them stiffen to the current where they stood. The woman's voice went on, sweet and deep and un-shaken:

'I don't suppose you men realise how much this—this sort of thing means to a woman. I've borne three. We women don't want our children given to Crowds. It must be an inherited instinct. Crowds make trouble. They bring back the Old Days. Hate, fear, blackmail, publicity, "The People"—That! That! That!' She pointed to the Statue, and the crowd growled once more.

'Yes, if they are allowed to go on,' said De Forest. 'But this little affair—'

'It means so much to us women that this—this little affair should never happen again. Of course, never's a big word, but one feels so strongly that it is important to stop crowds at the very beginning. Those creatures'—she pointed with her left hand at the prisoners swaying like seaweed in a tide way as the circuit pulled them—'those people have friends and wives and children in the city and elsewhere. One doesn't want anything done to them, you know. It's terrible to force a human being out of fifty or sixty years of good life. I'm only forty myself. I know. But, at the same time, one feels that an example should be made, because no price is too heavy to pay if—if these people and all that they imply can be put an end to. Do you quite understand or would you be kind enough to tell your men to take the casing off the Statue? It's worth looking at.'

'I understand perfectly. But I don't think anybody here wants to see the Statue on an empty stomach. Excuse me one moment.' De Forest called up to the ship, 'A flying loop ready on the port side, if you please.' Then to the woman he said with some crispness, 'You might leave us a little discretion in the matter.'

'Oh, of course. Thank you for being so patient.

I know my arguments are silly, but—' She half turned away and went on in a changed voice, 'Perhaps this will help you to decide.'

She threw out her right arm with a knife in it. Before the blade could be returned to her throat or her bosom it was twitched from her grip, sparked as it flew out of the shadow of the ship above, and fell flashing in the sunshine at the foot of the Statue fifty yards away. The outflung arm was arrested, rigid as a bar for an instant, till the releasing circuit permitted her to bring it slowly to her side. The other women shrank back silent among the men.

Pirolo rubbed his hands, and Takahira nodded.

'That was clever of you, De Forest,' said he.

'What a glorious pose!' Dragomiroff murmured, for the frightened woman was on the edge of tears.

'Why did you stop me? I would have done it!' she cried.

'I have no doubt you would,' said De Forest. 'But we can't waste a life like yours on these people. I hope the arrest didn't sprain your wrist; it's so hard to regulate a flying loop. But I think you are quite right about those persons' women and children. We'll take them all away with us if you promise not to do anything stupid to yourself.'

'I promise—I promise.' She controlled herself

with an effort. 'But it is so important to us women. We know what it means; and I thought if you saw I was in earnest—'

'I saw you were, and you've gained your point. I shall take all your Serviles away with me at once. The Mayor will make lists of their friends and families in the city and the district, and he'll ship them after us this afternoon.'

'Sure,' said the Mayor, rising to his feet. 'Keefe, if you can see, hadn't you better finish levelling off the Old Market? It don't look sightly the way it is now, and we shan't use it for crowds any more.'

'I think you had better wipe out that Statue as well, Mr. Mayor,' said De Forest. 'I don't question its merits as a work of art, but I believe it's a shade morbid.'

'Certainly, sir. Oh, Keefe! Slag the Nigger before you go on to fuse the Market. I'll get to the Communicators and tell the District that the Board is in charge. Are you making any special appointments, sir?'

'None. We haven't men to waste on these backwoods. Carry on as before, but under the Board. Arnott, run your Serviles aboard, please. Ground ship and pass them through the bilge-doors. We'll wait till we've finished with this work of art.'

The prisoners trailed past him, talking fluently, but unable to gesticulate in the drag of the current. Then the surfacers rolled up, two on each side of the Statue. With one accord the spectators looked elsewhere, but there was no need. Keefe turned on full power, and the thing simply melted within its case. All I saw was a surge of white-hot metal pouring over the plinth, a glimpse of Salati's inscription, 'To the Eternal Memory of the Justice of the People,' ere the stone base itself cracked and powdered into finest lime. The crowd cheered.

'Thank you,' said De Forest; but we want our breakfasts, and I expect you do too. Good-bye, Mr. Mayor! Delighted to see you at any time, but I hope I shan't have to, officially, for the next thirty years. Good-bye, madam. Yes. We're all given to nerves nowadays. I suffer from them myself. Good-bye, gentlemen all! You're under the tyrannous heel of the Board from this moment, but if ever you feel like breaking your fetters you've only to let us know. This is no treat to us. Good luck!'

We embarked amid shouts, and did not check our lift till they had dwindled into whispers. Then De Forest flung himself on the chart room divan and mopped his forehead.

'I don't mind men,' he panted, 'but women are the devil!'

'Still the devil,' said Pirolo cheerfully. 'That one would have suicided.'

'I know it. That was why I signalled for the flying loop to be clapped on her. I owe you an apology for that, Arnott. I hadn't time to catch your eye, and you were busy with our caitiffs. By the way, who actually answered my signal? It was a smart piece of work.'

'Ilroy,' said Arnott; 'but he overloaded the wave. It may be pretty gallery-work to knock a knife out of a lady's hand, but didn't you notice how she rubbed 'em? He scorched her fingers. Slovenly, I call it.'

'Far be it from me to interfere with Fleet discipline, but don't be too hard on the boy. If that woman had killed herself they would have killed every Servile and everything related to a Servile throughout the district by nightfall.'

'That was what she was playing for,' Takahira said. 'And with our Fleet gone we could have done nothing to hold them.'

'I may be ass enough to walk into a ground-circuit,' said Arnott, 'but I don't dismiss my Fleet till I'm reasonably sure that trouble is over. They're in position still, and I intend to keep 'em there till the Serviles are shipped out of the district. That last little crowd meant murder, my friends.'

'Nerves! All nerves!' said Pirolo. 'You cannot argue with agoraphobia.'

'And it is not as if they had seen much dead—or is it?' said Takahira.

'In all my ninety years I have never seen death.' Dragomiroff spoke as one who would excuse himself. 'Perhaps that was why—last night—'

Then it came out as we sat over breakfast, that, with the exception of Arnott and Pirolo, none of us had ever seen a corpse, or knew in what manner the spirit passes.

'We're a nice lot to flap about governing the Planet,' De Forest laughed. 'I confess, now it's all over, that my main fear was I mightn't be able to pull it off without losing a life.'

'I thought of that too,' said Arnott; 'but there's no death reported, and I've inquired everywhere. What are we supposed to do with our passengers? I've fed 'em.'

'We're between two switches,' De Forest drawled. 'If we drop them in any place that isn't under the Board, the natives will make their presence an excuse for cutting out, same as Illinois did, and forcing the Board to take over. If we drop them in any place under the Board's control they'll be killed as soon as our backs are turned.'

'If you say so,' said Pirolo thoughtfully, 'I can guarantee that they will become extinct in process of time, quite happily. What is their birth-rate now?'

'Go down and ask 'em,' said De Forest.

'I think they might become nervous and tear

me to bits,' the philosopher of Foggia replied.

'Not really? Well?'

'Open the bilge-doors,' said Takahira with a downward jerk of the thumb.

'Scarcely—after all the trouble we've taken to save 'em,' said De Forest.

'Try London,' Arnott suggested. 'You could turn Satan himself loose there, and they'd only ask him to dinner.'

'Good man! You've given me an idea. Vincent! Oh, Vincent!' He threw the General Communicator open so that we could all hear, and in a few minutes the chartroom filled with the rich, fruity voice of Leopold Vincent, who has purveyed all London her choicest amusements for the last thirty years. We answered with expectant grins, as though we were actually in the stalls of, say, the Combination on a first night.

'We've picked up something in your line,' De Forest began.

'That's good, dear man. if it's old enough. There's nothing to beat the old things for business purposes. Have you seen London, Chatham, and Dover at Earl's Court? No? I thought I missed you there. Im-mense! I've had the real steam locomotive engines built from the old designs and the iron rails cast specially by hand. Cloth cushions in the carriages, too! Im-mense! And paper railway tickets. And Polly Milton.'

'Polly Milton back again!' said Arnott rapturously. 'Book me two stalls for to-morrow night. What's she singing now, bless her?'

'The old songs. Nothing comes up to the old touch. Listen to this, dear men.' Vincent carolled with flourishes:

Oh, cruel lamps of London,

If tears your light could drown,

Your victims' eyes would weep them,

Oh, lights of London Town!

Then they weep.'

'You see?' Pirolo waved his hands at us. 'The old world always weeped when it saw crowds together. It did not know why, but it weeped. We know why, but we do not weep, except when we pay to be made to by fat, wicked old Vincent.'

'Old, yourself!' Vincent laughed. 'I'm a public benefactor, I keep the world soft and united.'

'And I'm De Forest of the Board,' said De Forest acidly, 'trying to get a little business done. As I was saying, I've picked up a few people in Chicago.'

'I cut out. Chicago is—'

'Do listen! They're perfectly unique.'

'Do they build houses of baked mud blocks while you wait—eh? That's an old contact.'

'They're an untouched primitive community, with all the old ideas.'

'Sewing-machines and maypole-dances? Cooking on coal-gas stoves, lighting pipes with matches, and driving horses? Gerolstein tried that last year. An absolute blow-out!'

De Forest plugged him wrathfully, and poured out the story of our doings for the last twenty-four hours on the top-note.

'And they do it all in public,' he concluded. 'You can't stop 'em. The more public, the better they are pleased. They'll talk for hours—like you! Now you can come in again!'

'Do you really mean they know how to vote?' said Vincent. 'Can they act it?'

'Act? It's their life to 'em! And you never saw such faces! Scarred like volcanoes. Envy, hatred, and malice in plain sight. Wonderfully flexible voices. They weep, too.'

'Aloud? In public?'

'I guarantee. Not a spark of shame or reticence in the entire installation. It's the chance of your career.'

'D'you say you've brought their voting props along—those papers and ballot-box things?'

'No, confound you! I'm not a luggage-lifter. Apply direct to the Mayor of Chicago. He'll forward you everything. Well?'

'Wait a minute. Did Chicago want to kill 'em? That 'ud look well on the Communicators.'

'Yes! They were only rescued with difficulty from a howling mob—if you know what that is.'

'But I don't,' answered the Great Vincent simply.

'Well then, they'll tell you themselves. They can make speeches hours long.'

'How many are there?'

'By the time we ship 'em all over they'll be perhaps a hundred, counting children. An old world in miniature. Can't you see it?'

'M—yes; but I've got to pay for it if it's a blow-out, dear man.'

'They can sing the old war songs in the streets. They can get word-drunk, and make crowds, and invade privacy in the genuine old-fashioned way; and they'll do the voting trick as often as you ask 'em a question.'

'Too good!' said Vincent.

'You unbelieving Jew! I've got a dozen head aboard here. I'll put you through direct. Sample 'em yourself.'

He lifted the switch and we listened. Our passengers on the lower deck at once, but not less than five at a time, explained themselves to Vincent. They had been taken from the bosom of their families, stripped of their possessions, given food without finger-bowls, and cast into captivity in a noisome dungeon.

'But look here,' said Arnott aghast; 'they're saying what isn't true. My lower deck isn't noisome, and I saw to the finger-bowls myself.'

'My people talk like that sometimes in Little Russia,' said Dragomiroff. 'We reason with them. We never kill. No!'

'But it's not true,' Arnott insisted. 'What can you do with people who don't tell facts? They're mad!'

'Hsh!' said Pirolo, his hand to his ear. 'It is such a little time since all the Planet told lies.'

We heard Vincent silkily sympathetic. Would they, he asked, repeat their assertions in public— before a vast public? Only let Vincent give them a chance, and the Planet, they vowed, should ring with their wrongs. Their aim in life—two women and a man explained it together—was to reform the world. Oddly enough, this also had been Vincent's life-dream. He offered them an arena in which to explain, and by their living example to raise the Planet to loftier levels. He was eloquent on the moral uplift of a simple, old-world life presented in its entirety to a deboshed civilisation.

Could they—would they—for three months certain, devote themselves under his auspices, as missionaries, to the elevation of mankind at a place called Earl's Court, which he said, with some truth, was one of the intellectual centres of the Planet? They thanked him, and demanded (we could hear his chuckle of delight) time to discuss and to vote on the matter. The vote, solemnly managed by counting heads—one head, one vote—was favourable. His offer, therefore, was accepted, and they moved a vote of thanks to him in two speeches—one by what they called the 'proposer' and the other by the 'seconder.'

Vincent threw over to us, his voice shaking with gratitude:

'I've got 'em! Did you hear those speeches? That's Nature, dear men. Art can't teach that. And they voted as easily as lying. I've never had a troupe of natural liars before. Bless you, dear men! Remember, you're on my free lists for ever, anywhere—all of you. Oh, Gerolstein will be sick—sick!'

'Then you think they'll do?' said De Forest.

'Do? The Little Village'll go crazy! I'll knock up a series of old-world plays for 'em. Their voices will make you laugh and cry. My God, dear men, where do you suppose they picked up all their misery from, on this sweet earth? I'll have a pageant of the world's beginnings, and Mosenthal shall do the music. I'll—'

'Go and knock up a village for 'em by to-night. We'll meet you at No. 15 West Landing Tower,' said De Forest. 'Remember the rest will be coming along to-morrow.'

'Let 'em all come!' said Vincent. 'You don't know how hard it is nowadays even for me, to find something that really gets under the public's damned iridium-plated hide. But I've got it at last. Good-bye!'

'Well,' said De Forest when we had finished laughing, 'if any one understood corruption in London I might have played off Vincent against Gerolstein, and sold my captives at enormous prices. As it is, I shall have to be their legal adviser to-night when the contracts are signed. And they won't exactly press any commission on me, either.'

'Meantime,' said Takahira, 'we cannot, of course, confine members of Leopold Vincent's last-engaged company. Chairs for the ladies, please, Arnott.'

'Then I go to bed,' said De Forest. 'I can't face any more women!' And he vanished.

When our passengers were released and given another meal (finger-bowls came first this time) they told us what they thought of us and the Board; and, like Vincent, we all marvelled how they had contrived to extract and secrete so much bitter poison and unrest out of the good life God gives us. They raged, they stormed, they palpitated, flushed and exhausted their poor, torn nerves, panted themselves into silence, and renewed the senseless, shameless attacks.

'But can't you understand,' said Pirolo pathetically to a shrieking woman, 'that if we'd left you in

Chicago you'd have been killed?'

'No, we shouldn't. You were bound to save us from being murdered.'

'Then we should have had to kill a lot of other people.'

'That doesn't matter. We were preaching the Truth. You can't stop us. We shall go on preaching in London; and then you'll see!'

'You can see now,' said Pirolo, and opened a lower shutter.

We were closing on the Little Village, with her three Million people spread out at ease inside her ring of girdling Main-Traffic lights—those eight fixed beams at Chatham, Tonbridge, Redhill, Dorking, Woking, St. Albans, Chipping Ongar, and Southend.

Leopold Vincent's new company looked, with small pale faces, at the silence, the size, and the separated houses.

Then some began to weep aloud, shamelessly—always without shame.

"MacDonough's Song"

Whether the State can loose and bind
In Heaven as well as on Earth:
If it be wiser to kill mankind
Before or after the birth—
These are matters of high concern
Where State-kept school men are;
But Holy State (we have lived to learn)
Endeth in Holy War.

Whether The People be led by the Lord,
Or lured by the loudest throat:
If it be quicker to die by the sword
Or cheaper to die by vote—
These are the things we have dealt with once,
(And they will not rise from their grave)
For Holy People, however it runs,
Endeth in wholly Slave.

Rudyard Kipling's WITH THE NIGHT MAIL

Whatsoever, for any cause,
  Seeketh to take or give,
Power above or beyond the Laws,
  Suffer it not to live!
Holy State or Holy King—
  Or Holy People's Will—
Have no truck with the senseless thing.
  Order the guns and kill!

  Saying—after—me:—

Once there was The People —Terror gave it birth;
Once there was The People and it made a Hell of Earth.
Earth arose and crushed it. Listen, O ye slain!
Once there was The People—it shall never be again!

Down With the People
Afterword by Bruce Sterling

WHEN RUDYARD KIPLING WROTE these prescient and truly extraor-
dinary stories, the term "science fiction" was still twenty years un-
born. Why did Kipling do it?

The simplest answer is that Rudyard Kipling could publish anything he could dream up. During the golden period of these stories, 1905-1912, Kipling was about as famous as it was possible for
a writer to get. The English public worshipped him. The American
public admired him, even though he picked conspicuous fights with
them. Mark Twain thought the world of him. Henry James was the
best man at his wedding. Kipling had just won the Nobel Prize for
Literature. If there were worlds left for him to conquer, they were
in writing things that no previous writer could even dream about.

Kipling had already published some exceedingly well-received
stories about steamships and railroads. Like most Kipling tales, these
stories were crammed with snappy jargon, dramatic events and well-
researched technical details. So why not take that writerly ability,
and turn it to the topic of, say, futuristic super-dirigibles? Everybody
knew that flying airships were coming, because the newspapers in
1905 were full of that news. All it took was the boldness to make that
conceptual leap.

All the snappy jargon would be faked. The dramatic events would
be incredible happenstances that no human being had ever experienced, such as being wrapped in a big inflatable rubber air-suit and
having a meteor remove your electrical charge. Even the technical
details would be one long visionary parody of real-life technologies—mail delivery by a radium-powered aerial steamship-locomo-
tive that could fly around the world.

And, having succeeded at that feat of invention, why not up the
ante by teasing the magazine in which this story appeared? Do that
by making up—cruelly parodying, even—the contents of the magazine itself. Would the editors print this arch, mocking, self-conscious
contrivance—even though Kipling was making arrogant fun of the

whole tiresome business of getting published in a magazine? You bet they would print any Rudyard Kipling story. And they cheerfully did.

Fame fertilized Rudyard Kipling's eccentricities. This situation allowed him to anticipate science fiction. Rudyard Kipling, since his earliest youth, had been a notably eccentric guy. Although Kipling was alarmingly bright and even rather good-looking, he was also small, near-sighted and painfully sensitive to any trace of insult and disrespect. Fame therefore did him personal harm. Not because he gave into fame, but because he successfully fought it.

Kipling had married the sister of his American literary agent. Mrs. Kipling, a pragmatic and practical woman, knew rather a lot about the worldly worth of a successful writer of genius. When Kipling told her that he needed to be left alone in his study to work, she took this husbandly command with a lifelong seriousness. If Mr. Kipling wanted to be shut up alone in his office to dream and scribble, then in he would go, and in he would stay. Mrs. Kipling kept the prying world at bay—to the point of literally guarding her husband's office door with her own desk.

Since Kipling had once been a boy reporter for British-Indian newspapers, he commonly passed for a hardbitten, common-sensical man of the world. All his stories play up this self-image, the greatest of Kipling's many fictions. The Kipling narrator is always firmly on the side of our world's practical, no-nonsense people: the engineers, soldiers, sailors, policemen, and bossy moms. Kipling was in fact a craft-friendly guy, and pretty good with his hands—his dad was an architectural designer, while his uncle was a Pre-Raphaelite painter. So Kipling knew his way around a workbench and an atelier. He genuinely enjoyed chatting with Edwardian steam technicians, who, by the way, were also his most loyal fans.

Kipling enjoyed the challenge of making fine literature out of the most rugged, resistant aspects of material life—cannons, pistons, cogwheels, bridges, trenchworks. Kipling knew that this engagement with industrial modernity cut him out of the pack—those brainy, hand-waving cliques of effete critics, philosophers, professors, politicians, and, well, most writers other than himself.

But Kipling, who was a genius and never a simple personality, was not some omni-competent tough guy, but a near-sighted, prickly, jittery guy much given to ulcers and sudden nervous breakdowns. With his skyrocketing fancies and his fits of impulsive behavior, Kipling would have been one of the worst engineers or ship captains that one could imagine.

HiLoBooks

There aren't any genuinely Kipling-like people in the entire works of Kipling. Even his own posthumous autobiography isn't much like the real Kipling. The real Kipling was a desk-bound genius happily poring over arcane reference works while Mom brought in sandwiches. The real Kipling was a personality type that any modern science fiction fan would immediately recognize. He was your basic geek MENSA type, exceedingly bright, verbally fluent, polymathic and interested in literally everything, but hard-put to make any real friends. As he gets what he wants most from life—a workaholic splendor—he slowly drifts into a lonely isolation, and, with age, an ever-thickening political and social crankiness. Nobody can save him from that fate, because nobody is smart enough to talk sense to him on his own level.

With the Night Mail is an amazing tour-de-force of inspired genius—Kipling, in 1905, is doing things that science fiction as a genre wouldn't achieve until Robert Heinlein arrived in the late 1940s. Unlike Jules Verne (who was still beavering away on his own high-tech airship stories around 1905), Kipling doesn't explain anything. Or rather, Kipling does explain, but every "explanation" is cunningly framed in terms of being something else—it's a matter of money, a personal conflict, an illegal affront, an inside joke, a danger to shipping, a pretty curio. It's anything but dry and boring exposition about how a future aircraft works. And yet you see the whole machine there, literally stem to stern.

Most interesting of all, the story isn't even really a "story." There's scarcely a plot in it, and the characters are cardboard. *With the Night Mail* is "experiential futurism," a phony piece of a future magazine to be encountered while opening a genuine magazine. *With the Night Mail* was originally inserted inside a real magazine, rather in the way that J. G. Ballard liked to make up fake ads in issues of *Ambit* in the 1960s. *With the Night Mail* is therefore a hoax and a put-on. It's what postmodernists nowadays would call an "intervention." It's more than a mere work of popular fiction.

The profundity of this Kipling stunt doesn't come across well in book form—our magazines, what's left of them, no longer behave like his magazines. But it was exceedingly clever, the sort of thing that Verne or Wells would never have dreamed of doing. Even Robert Louis Stevenson couldn't have done it. Mark Twain might have done it. Twain knew Nikola Tesla personally, and Twain still thought that Kipling was probably the smartest guy in the world.

"As Easy as A.B.C." was something of a late sequel to *Night Mail*.

Rudyard Kipling's WITH THE NIGHT MAIL

It came along a full seven years later, after Kipling had worked with a historian and gotten interested in historical change. "A.B.C." is about historical changes in politics, or, rather, it's a visionary utopia where life has changed so much that politics are unnecessary.

In the "easy" world of "A.B.C.," everything is run by the practical technocrats whom Kipling professed to admire. Politics has died from lack of any sincere interest; there is no "society" any more, but only private individuals.

The Kipling of 1912 is as smart as the Kipling of 1905, but he's in a much worse mood. "A.B.C." shows a loathing of sociality—really, an unfeigned, shrinking fleshy horror of large numbers of people all standing in the same place. Reclusive but world-famous celebrities are commonly bugged by such things. "Privacy" seems to be the only civil right that matters in this future world. Kipling figures that he's making some terrific sense here, but he's working through some of his own worst personal anxieties. They're not pretty.

The persistent business about the hideous statue of the murdered black victim is especially unfortunate. Chicago's cruelty to black immigrants in 1912 wasn't any news to a perceptive observer from outside America. Kipling had married an American and lived and worked in America. He'd watched Americans pirating his work for years. He enjoyed this chance to loudly talk about rope in the house of the hanged man.

"A.B.C." is a crazy-making story—it's blatantly offensive in so many obvious ways, yet much more offensive once you start thinking seriously about its premises. What's more, "A.B.C." is mild stuff compared to another Kipling political provocation from the same period of his life, "The Mother Hive." In "Mother Hive," a royal sorority of sturdy, well-behaved talking bees are subverted, misled and destroyed by an evil feminist suffragette. "The Mother Hive" rehearses a number of cogent themes: racial decline, parasitism, secret cliques of breeding aliens, unthinkable intellectual perversions, gooey blind insect-monsters, loathsome inbred degeneracy... that H. P. Lovecraft would champion twenty years later. "The Mother Hive" out-Lovecrafts Lovecraft, and is a much better political story than "A.B.C."

However "A.B.C." certainly has many strong merits as a work of science fiction. The greatest merit of "A.B.C." is that the world it extrapolates is truly weird. It's so spacey that it's in some sense timeless. It's not a mere partisan fairy-story like "Mother Hive," but a truly radical future scenario.

The future world of A.B.C. fails to divide neatly on any kind of analytical or left-right divide. Instead it has the true surreality of a society transfixed and dominated by its own unconscious upheavals.

A.B.C. is full of oxymorons, of contradictions in terms. If this world is properly run by level-headed international technocrats (as the story assures us that it is), then why is the human race dying out? Wouldn't a practical person confront this issue, instead of languidly accepting it?

Why does the heroine of the story (at least, she's the only woman with any say whatsoever) attempt to commit suicide? Why is this martyr-operation of hers considered such a great thing, and such a bracing gesture of authenticity? When the story's political subversives are not killed (they expect to be killed) but instead, are turned into hugely profitable pop-culture stars—why is that a solution?

One might also note that this is a future society "without war." Yet the story opens with a strange crisis that is very like a so-called "cyberwar" attack. "Illinois had riotously cut itself out of all systems and would remain disconnected." The electrical power system is down, the roads and airports are closed. "All General Communications were dumb." In 2012, we fully get it about riot-stricken regions cutting themselves off from the Internet. "A.B.C." was written in 1912.

Consider the spooky non-lethal riot weaponry of the powers-that-be in "A.B.C."—lasers, sonic weapons and some taser-like paralysis rays, all delivered from above, NATO air-power style. The actual "Aerial Board of Control" must have seemed pretty far-fetched in 1912, but nowadays the A.B.C. seems almost routine. It's as powerful, as anonymous, as bored and as unhappy as the Internet Engineering Task Force. The IETF are another bunch of competent, responsible, international, Kiplingesque guys—just like the A.B.C., they are commonly complaining that they really didn't want such an important job, and they don't much know what to do with it.

The world of the Internet is wreathed in blazing controversy nowadays. Its technical masters, such as they are, come off like bright but detached people who would be far happier left alone in a studio, doing some genius coding. Boy, if only that would work out for us, hey? We can dream, can't we?

Just let them get on with the real work at hand! That's all they ask from the normal people! Just bring 'em a sandwich, that's all they really need! A sandwich, and maybe this book.